"Go away, Eric."

"I'm a guest here."

"Then go on up to the house. Leave me alone."

His reply was less irate than it was sorrowful. "Why, Mary?" He stopped a few feet from her. "Is it because of what happened in the past?"

"I don't know what you're talking about."

"That's it, isn't it?" Taking her arm, he stilled it and kept her from stepping away.

"Forget it, Eric. I have."

He shook his head. "How can I forget a time as beautiful as that?"

"Oh, spare me. Just do what you did then and kiss me off. It should be easy for you. You've had enough practice."

"Oh, for the love of..."

"*Love* had nothing to do with it. Now let me go."

"I can't let you go," he said, his slow, sensuous drawl reminiscent of nothing Mary had ever heard from him before.

Dear Reader,

These days, when it feels like winter just *might* last forever, don't forget—you can find all the warmth and magic of springtime anytime in a Silhouette Romance book.

Each month, Silhouette Romance brings you six captivating love stories. Share all the laughter, the tears and the tenderness as our spirited heroines and irresistible heroes discover the wonder and power of love.

This month, meet the dynamic Thatcher Brant, hero of *Haunted Husband*. The handsome widower has vowed he'll never love again. But Samantha Hogan is determined to break the spell of Thatcher's past and win his heart. It all happens in Elizabeth August's SMYTHESHIRE, MASSACHUSETTS, a small New England town with big secrets....

Thatcher is also a FABULOUS FATHER, part of our special series about very special dads.

Then there's *Sally's Beau,* Riley Houston. He's the footloose and fancy-free type, but Sally's out to show Riley there's world enough for this pair of ALL-AMERICAN SWEETHEARTS in Paradise Falls, West Virginia! Don't miss this heartwarming story from Laurie Paige.

Rounding out the month, there's Carla Cassidy's *The Golden Girl,* Gayle Kaye's *Hard Hat and Lace,* Val Whisenand's *Daddy's Back* and Anne Peters's sophisticated *The Pursuit of Happiness.*

In the coming months, we'll be bringing you books by all your favorite authors—Diana Palmer, Annette Broadrick, Suzanne Carey and more!

I hope you enjoy this book, and all the stories to come.

Happy Reading!

Anne Canadeo
Senior Editor

DADDY'S BACK
Val Whisenand

Silhouette
ROMANCE™
Published by Silhouette Books New York
America's Publisher of Contemporary Romance

Many thanks to Clydene Boots of Westview Farm
for all her help in the research
that went into this story

SILHOUETTE BOOKS
300 E. 42nd St., New York, N.Y. 10017

DADDY'S BACK

Copyright © 1993 by Valerie Whisenand

ISBN: 0-373-08926-0

First Silhouette Books printing March 1993

Books by Val Whisenand

Silhouette Romance

Treasure Hunters #655
Giveaway Girl #695
For Eternity #802
Molly Meets Her Match #890
Daddy's Back #926

VAL WHISENAND

is an incurable romantic, married to her high school sweetheart since she was seventeen. The mother of two grown children, she lives in a house she designed and that she and her husband built together. Her varied interests have led her to explore many fascinating occupations and travel throughout the United States and Canada. Whether her goal is to write another book, learn a foreign language or prevail over tremendous odds to become a winning game-show contestant, her natural tenacity sees to it that she succeeds. Once she makes up her mind, there's no stopping her!

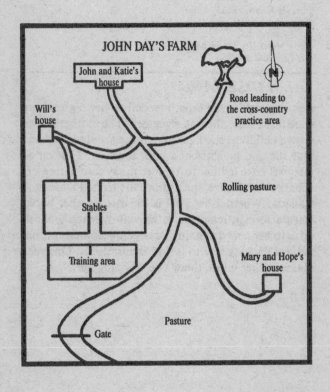

JOHN DAY'S FARM

John and Katie's house

Will's house

Road leading to the cross-country practice area

Stables

Rolling pasture

Training area

Mary and Hope's house

Gate

Pasture

Chapter One

Mary Mulraney pushed up the sleeves of her bulky Aran sweater, rested her elbows along the top rail of the fence and welcomed the rare warmth of the sun on her fair skin. California seemed so remote and far away it was easy to convince herself that part of her life was little more than a bad dream. Watching her seven-year-old daughter ride effortlessly across the lush, green pasture, she smiled with pride.

"I'd thought the chestnut was too much horse for her," Mary said to the gray-haired groom beside her, "but you were right, William."

He smiled back at her, his leathery face full of mirth beneath the visor of his tweed cap. "The girl can fairly ride."

"Well, you needn't look so pleased."

"Not as pleased as you."

Mary leaned forward, a familiar wistfulness flowing through her. "She is a wonder, isn't she?"

"Aye. You named her well."

"Hope? Yes." She nodded her head slowly, her coppery-blond hair swinging in soft waves. The child had been her only hope of happiness for so long that the name seemed preordained. None other was worth considering. The fact that Mary had kept the family name of Mulraney for them both did bother her some, though. It would have been nicer to have legitimatized the child with a father's surname. Still, as long as Hope never learned the truth, what was the harm?

Mary's hands gripped the fence rail, her blue eyes widening. "Oh, no. Not again." She glanced at William for only a split second. "Look at her! I've told her and told her, yet she insists on jumping." Holding her breath, she let it out in a whoosh as Hope's mount landed effortlessly on the far side of a split-rail jump a hundred yards away.

"She's your daughter. It's in her blood."

Mary nodded and sighed. Superior horsemanship *was* in Hope's blood, in more ways than one. Her father was a world champion, and Mary herself, had once been considered up-and-coming in international competitive circles. Therefore Hope's slim, athletic build and natural ability was a given. The pity was that she could never be allowed to ride professionally.

As if reading Mary's thoughts, the old groom nudged her shoulder. "She should be taught proper techniques."

"No! I've told you . . ." Seeing the hurt in his expression, she tempered the intensity of her reaction. "As long as Hope is safe, that's all I want."

"It may be what *you* want but it's not what the girl wants." He gestured. Hope was galloping rapidly toward a low stone wall. "Look there. Now watch. See how she leans into the jump? 'Tis a talent you can't deny."

"I know, William." Mary's heart lurched and her stomach knotted with the memory of another who rode and jumped as effortlessly, as gracefully as the child. The older

Hope got, the more she reminded Mary of Eric, damn him. Astride one of the horses at John Day's farm, Hope became a vivid reminder of her father. Of Mary's youthful foolishness. Of the most painful rejection of her life. Clenching her jaw, Mary welcomed the anger that coursed through her, taking the place of sweeter remembrances of the man who'd once meant everything to her.

"But I'll never let Hope start competing, so you and Uncle John might just as well give up trying to convince me otherwise," Mary said flatly. "It's no fit life for a child, all that traveling and loneliness. My daughter has a true home like I never did. I've seen to that, thanks to Uncle John. And by the saints, I'll see she stays safely in it."

"Even if it breaks her heart?"

Mary's blue eyes snapped up to meet the serious gray depths of the old man's. "It won't break her heart the way the riding circuit can. She'll not go out there among the vultures to be pushed and prodded till she doesn't know who her real friends are or where her next bed will be. It's no proper life for an adult, let alone a tender child."

The old man nodded solemnly. "You were cut deep, eh, girl?"

"To the heart, William. My daughter will not have to go through that as long as I have breath in my body." Turning away, Mary walked stiffly back toward the stables. It was beginning to rain.

The Irish countryside was much more beautiful than Eric Lambert had expected it to be. Moreover, it had a kind of inherent peacefulness to it that was beginning to relax him.

"This is The Curragh," the cab driver called back over his right shoulder. "And up the road at Tully is the National Stud. You plannin' on seein' it, too?"

"Perhaps later," Eric said. "It depends on how my business with Mr. Day goes."

"A fine man," the driver observed.

"Yes." It would be a pleasure to see John Day again. In their recent telephone conversations, he'd tempted Eric with a proposal too sweet to pass up. The only question was, why? Their earlier association was pleasant enough but hardly warranted such open handedness.

Eric leaned forward to peer out the cab's window. A country lane bisected the pastures to the left. At the end of the narrow track rose a massive, gray stone house. Rain drops and condensation on the glass began to obscure his view, so he cranked the window down. Cool, damp air as fresh and clean as he'd ever tasted drifted in.

"I'll drive you around front, sir."

"Yes. Thanks. I . . ." Out of the corner of his eye, Eric spotted a magnificent horse. Its rider was so small he had to look twice before he was certain his mind wasn't playing tricks on him. "Wait!"

The rider was not a jockey as he'd first imagined, but was, instead, a young girl. The elusive thought that he'd seen her somewhere before darted through his mind and was gone as quickly as it came. Galloping at a right angle to the lane, she headed straight for the high fences that bordered it. Dear Lord, it looked as if she intended to jump. Even if she made it over the first fence, there would be no time to turn before hitting the second, and to attempt a combination jump with so little space between was more than a dangerous folly. It was impossible.

Eric's hands tightened on the back of the seat. The stupid kid was actually going to try it. If she wasn't killed herself, she'd probably ruin the horse. And the cab was stopped too far away for him to run out and warn her. Hell, she wasn't even wearing a protective helmet!

Never missing a stride, the horse gathered beneath the child in response to her body language. Eric instinctively leaned and flexed with her. The horse's muscles bunched, its stride lengthened, and it was airborne, sailing over the rails of the left-hand fence as if it were no more trouble than traversing the gently sloping pasture.

In a heartbeat, the horse's front hooves touched the ground, its rear legs followed, and it once again leaped, easily clearing the right-hand fence. In seconds, both horse and rider had vanished down the hill, disappearing behind a curtain of Irish mist.

With a guttural exclamation Eric sank back against the car seat and ran his fingers through his thick, dark hair. If he hadn't seen it, he wouldn't have believed it. Such jumps were the stuff legends were made of. And that child . . .

"How in the hell did she do that?" he muttered.

"She's an Irish lass on an Irish horse." Grinning, the driver looked around. "I'm not at all surprised."

Speechless, Eric waved him on. As the car picked up speed, he pictured the beautiful child and the fantastic jumping he'd just witnessed. They were a magnificent pair, the chestnut and its rider, so in tune with each other that they'd become one, both in action and in spirit.

He snorted in disgust. Horsemanship was one thing, stupidity was another. Whoever that girl's parents were, they should be chastised for permitting her to take such chances. That was exactly the kind of foolish stunt that gave sports like Three-Day Eventing or steeplechase a bad name. Worse, the incident had apparently occurred on John Day's property.

Eric wondered if he'd made a mistake in agreeing to come all this way to negotiate with the man. He hoped not. He'd had his eye on the Day line of Caledon-bred horses for a long time. With his skills and a few selected members of

Caledon's offspring, he knew he'd have good luck breeding Irish stamina into his own horses. Beyond that, he told himself, he should have no other concerns.

Yet the child's daredevil jumping still bothered him. It would be a terrible waste to have such a promising rider sidelined because of injury. Or worse. He'd seen it happen too often. Even if it hurt his chances in dealing with Day, he was going to have to at least mention what he'd observed. His conscience insisted.

"It's mizzlin' again," Hope said. Throwing her leg over the saddle and kicking loose from the stirrups, she slid to the ground while William held the horse's bridle.

"Wouldn't be Ireland without rain," Mary countered. Bending to give and receive a kiss of greeting she tousled the girl's reddish-blond curls, darker than usual because they were so damp.

"I like a soft day." Hope's hazel eyes twinkled. "And Mr. O'Malley is in grand spirits."

Mary eyed the chestnut gelding. Hope had taken a liking to him when she'd seen him being born. Scarcely two years old at the time, the child had practically grown up with the animal and formed a bond that defied explanation. It was Hope who'd christened him Mr. O'Malley, after a favorite neighbor, and Mary had to agree with the choice of names. Both O'Malleys had rich brown hair, were high-spirited and handsome and lacked the brains God gave a goat.

The stupid horse would do anything Hope asked without hesitation, while a more levelheaded animal would balk or at least use good sense about trying. Someday, Mary feared, Mr. O'Malley and Hope were going to take a bad fall.

"I told you, I don't want you jumping him over such difficult obstacles, especially when it's raining," Mary cautioned.

"I know." Hope hung her head for the requisite several seconds before looking up with a broad, self-satisfied smile. "But it's *always* raining."

Behind Mary, William chuckled. "She's got you there."

"Hush up, old man," Mary told him with the scowl she'd first focused on Hope. "How do you expect me to scold the child effectively if you supply excuses for her all the time?"

"I'll go with William and help rub down Mr. O'Malley," Hope interjected, trotting along beside the horse.

The slim seven-year-old barely came to the horse's chest and Mary's old feelings of dread and worry surfaced. "Wait for me, Hope Mulraney. You and I aren't finished talking."

"Oh, Mama. I'm safe when I ride. You know Mr. O'Malley would never hurt me."

"Mr. O'Malley is a blithering idiot and he loves you so much he'd jump the moon if you asked him to."

The girl's expressive eyes widened beneath her long, thick lashes. "Do you think so?"

Mary couldn't help smiling, especially since William was laughing again. She was about to comment further when the telephone in the main barn jangled.

She threw her hands in the air in frustration. "Oh, never mind. That's probably Katie calling us up to the house for some of her soda bread. Brush the fool horse. I'll answer the phone."

Reaching the barn by crossing the paddock, she shook droplets of rain from her shoulder-length hair as she lifted the receiver and affected a perfect imitation of William's lilting brogue. "'Tis the mother of Mr. O'Malley's best friend speakin'. Say your piece." The deep, friendly chuckle on the other end of the line surprised her. Instead of her aunt Katie, the caller was Uncle John.

"I swear, Mary, you sound more Irish every time I talk to you."

She snorted. "Oh, do I? Seems to me I remember you teasing me about what you called my California-surfer accent a while back. You're a hard man to please."

"I am not. But let's not discuss my faults, for now. I have a business associate here to see Caledon."

The big stallion was, among other things, Mr. O'Malley's sire. He had more heart than any horse Mary had ever known, and she loved him for the sheer joy of watching and caring for so magnificent an animal.

Suddenly nervous about his future, she gripped the receiver more tightly. "You're not planning on selling him!"

"No, no. The gentleman simply wishes to see him. We'd discussed getting together the last time I visited the States and now he's come." John paused. "You spent enough years in competition that you probably met this client, yourself. The name's Lambert."

"*Eric* Lambert?" Mary's voice was little more than a squeak.

"Yes. I'm sure you've heard me mention him from time to time."

"No! Uh, yes. I mean, I guess I read about his success in the Olympics or something."

"Probably. He was in the stadium jumping competition we caught on satellite a few weeks ago. You missed his ride when you left the room. I remember he also won a bronze in Seoul in '88 and did well at the Pan-American Three-Day Event Championships in Georgia in '91." John paused briefly to take a breath. "But I'm rambling. Sorry. Get Caledon warmed up for us, will you? Mr. Lambert would like to see him work."

"Of course. Sure. Right away." Mary hung up the phone with a trembling hand. Eric. Oh, dear God, what heinous sin had she committed to bring such disaster down on her poor head? All the care and subterfuge she'd used to avoid watching his performance on television had been for nothing. Eric was in Ireland!

Gathering her wits about her, she dashed back to where William and Hope were currying the gelding.

"William! Stop that for now and get Caledon ready. Mr. John has a customer come to see him." She snatched the brush out of Hope's left hand while pulling her toward the stall door. "And don't mention me by name, do you hear? No gab. Hold your tongue for once." The puzzled look on his weathered countenance drew her up short. "I'll explain later. It's important. Please?"

He nodded, tipping his tweed cap. "Aye."

Mary continued to drag her daughter along in spite of the child's efforts to extricate herself. Two big yellow-striped barn cats darted out of her way.

"I'm not done," Hope whined.

"Yes, you are. William will finish up." She focused her attention on the old man's concerned expression. "Hope and I both have to go. I'll send Pat up to help you, if you like."

William raised one bushy eyebrow, left Mr. O'Malley's stall and followed her to the door. "Do whatever you must," he said slowly, questioningly.

Facing him, Mary drew a shaky breath. "I am, dear William. I am." She glanced down at the confused child beside her. "I always have."

Chapter Two

Mary and Hope's house had once served as the gardener's cottage. When the estate had been in its heyday, the stone mansion had belonged to the titled gentry while their Irish servants had lived apart in quaint, thatched-roof dwellings.

When she had arrived from the United States, pregnant and barely tolerating her parents' lie about her widowhood, her aunt and uncle had given her the option of choosing her own living quarters, and she had decided on the small but homey cottage, filling it with bits and pieces of whatever eclectic furnishings pleased her. In the ensuing years, she'd never been sorry. The cottage was the first place she'd ever lived that felt the way she imagined a home was supposed to.

"Go straighten up your room," Mary told Hope, taking her by the shoulders and urging her forward.

"Why?"

"Because I said so."

"Because I was jumping?"

Trembling with nervousness, Mary realized how gruff and unreasonable her commands must have sounded. She crouched down to be on the same level as her daughter and smoothed back the soft curls clustered around the child's rosy cheeks. "It was time to come home. That's all. You're not in trouble." Her reward was an angelic smile.

"I'm not?"

Mary sighed. "No, you're not. Though you should be. I understand how you love to ride. I even know how wonderful it feels to jump a good horse." Remembering, she hesitated. "It's just like flying."

The child nodded vigorously. "I thought I was the only one who knew that!"

Smiling, Mary hugged her tightly. "It'll be our secret, okay? If we tell, then everyone will want to do it."

Hope hugged her in return, little arms squeezing her neck, and placed a brief kiss on her mother's cheek. "I like secrets. Especially fun ones."

Forcing her smile to continue in spite of her churning stomach and wobbly legs, Mary disengaged the thin arms and stood. "Good. Now go clean up your room. Maybe we'll go for a walk later."

"But . . . Mr. O'Malley needs more brushing. We weren't finished when you made me leave."

"I already told you William will take care of the horse. That's his job."

"But he has to get Caledon for Uncle John."

"Then he'll have Pat or one of the other men see to it."

"But—"

"No buts," Mary ordered. "You know what I expect you to do."

Head hanging and feet scuffing the floor, the seven-year-old went to her room and slammed the door closed behind her, leaving Mary alone. Secrets. It took the uncluttered mind of a child to look upon secrets as things to be desired. Adult secrets were another matter.

Mary went slowly to the window and peered out through one of the small, rectangular panes. It was still a soft day. The rain was more a mist than anything. Her heavy sweater had kept her dry so that only the lower part of her jeans and her hair showed any effects of the moisture.

Sighing, she pushed waves of her unruly hair back off her forehead and noticed that her hands were still trembling. She held them out before her. Eric's presence had always affected her thusly. Even when she'd loved him from afar and he hadn't known or cared who she was, she'd literally quaked in her boots. Then, when he'd finally noticed and they'd made such beautiful love...

Mary pressed her fingertips to her lips, remembering. She'd been so happy, so excited, the next morning. All her dreams had come true. Eric loved her. She was his. She really belonged to someone after so many lonely years.

Tears misted her vision like the Irish rain on the fields. She'd awakened that day expecting Eric to be full of plans for their future, just as she was. The sweetly pungent, remembered aroma of the fresh straw seemed as real as his love had.

Tickling his tan, well-muscled chest with a piece of the straw, she'd snuggled closer. "Good morning, sleepyhead."

He'd jumped up and moved away from her as if she were some loathsome creature he'd just discovered under a rock.

"Mary, I don't know what to say." He tucked his shirttail into the waist of his jeans. "I mean... Oh, hell."

She got to her feet and followed him over to the ailing horse they had both tended during the night. He was bending down to check the animal's injured leg, but when he straightened he still didn't look at her.

"Eric. Please don't be angry with me."

He whirled, his green eyes blazing. "Angry with you? Good Lord, Mary, you're the one who should be furious." Rolling his gaze to the ceiling, he drew a shaky breath. "We were just friends. I never should have . . . I am so sorry."

A tear rolled down Mary's cheek just as it had over eight years before. Eric was sorry. She was elated, ready to begin a new life with the man she loved, and he was *sorry!* For loving her. For making her a woman. She'd expected love and he'd given her words of excuse, of embarrassment for losing control.

Feeling every bit as bereft as she had then, Mary raised her chin with pride and stared out at the green countryside. Well, so be it. The anger that had begun to burn that summer morning was even more potent now. Damn him. Let him be sorry. She wasn't.

Folding her arms around herself, she stood more straight. Even when she'd found out she carried his baby she hadn't been sorry. Far from it. Eric Lambert didn't know it, but he'd given her a part of himself to keep forever. He'd given her Hope.

Even though he was taller and a lot slimmer than John, Eric was glad he'd accepted the offer of the loan of a wool cap and jacket. If this was how it felt in summer, he'd hate to be in Ireland during the winter months. He shivered.

John clapped him on the shoulder. "I supposed you'd take a chill in this weather. California's a bit more on the dry side, I recall."

Nodding, Eric buttoned the jacket. "Even in wet years it's nothing like this. Everything is so *green* here."

"It wouldn't dare not be," John said pleasantly. Motioning to the old groom, he led Eric out to the paddock. "Mr. Lambert . . . Caledon."

The horse was as well-built and superbly conditioned as Eric had expected, even though he was getting on in years. Approaching with John's permission, Eric nodded to the groom, let Caledon sniff his hand, then proceeded to go over the entire animal by touch. Bending, he ran one hand down the foreleg to the pastern and lifted the hoof.

"Do you have someone who could ride him for me; put him through his paces?" he asked, straightening and patting Caledon's shoulder.

John glanced at William, then past him to the main barn. "My niece has been working him to keep him in shape. She's around here somewhere. Will, have you seen Mary?"

The old man immediately burst into a fit of coughing so severe that Caledon tossed his big head and tried to break away.

Clapping the groom on the back, John relieved him of the horse's lead rope, then passed control to Eric as he guided the coughing, wheezing man aside. "Will, for heaven's sake. What's wrong? Are you ill?"

"Aye. That must be it," he gasped between spasms. "I'm ill. Whilst I rest and get me breath, why not let Mr. Lambert try the horse himself?"

John paused, a puzzled look on his face. "You must be ill, Will Murphy. I don't believe I've ever heard you suggest a stranger ride one of our horses before."

Seating himself on a bale of bedding straw, the groom took off his cap and squeezed it in one of his big, callused hands. "There's times when a man sees what's best to be done and rules be hanged," he muttered. More loudly he added, "Mr. Lambert's well known. Surely he's sat a good horse before. Caledon will be none the worse for it."

Chuckling at the obscure logic of the statement, John lifted his head and spoke to Eric. "Well, you heard William. The horse is yours to ride. All I ask is that you not jump him without prior permission as to the course you intend to take."

Unable to believe the exchange he'd just witnessed, Eric drew John aside. "You *are* John Day, the owner of this farm, aren't you? I mean, since when does a groom tell you what to do?"

John laughed boisterously and cocked his head. "That old man practically raised me. If he wants you to ride Caledon, then it's all right with me. We're more like family here than owner and staff. The feudal system went out with the Middle Ages."

"I'm not questioning your decision," Eric quickly explained. "When you first contacted me, I'd hoped I'd get the chance to work Caledon, as well as inspect the rest of your stock, but confidentially, the ease of it took me by surprise." He smiled over at William, who was scowling back at him. "I'm still not sure he really means it, though. He's looking at me as if he wishes Caledon would kick me into the next county."

John laced his fingers together and bent by the horse's side to give Eric a leg up. As the younger man settled himself in the saddle and took up the reins, John smiled up at him. "The Irish are protective of their own—clannish, if you will—be it horse or friend. That's all that's bothering him. Enjoy your ride."

Nodding to both men, Eric swung Caledon away and into a peppy walk. He'd passed some outlying buildings and sloping terrain on his way to the big house. The narrow dirt paths between them would be a perfect, safe place to exercise the magnificent stallion.

He nudged Caledon's flanks and the horse responded fluidly and effortlessly. Eric's international flight had been long and tedious. The peace and natural beauty of the farm were so overwhelming, the horse so easy to handle, Eric was lulled almost immediately into a deeply relaxed mental state, not unlike euphoria.

Luckily, Caledon was more alert. Eric didn't see the child blocking the path ahead, but the horse did, dodging and skidding to a stop just in time to avoid an accident. A lesser horseman would have been unseated. With a muttered oath, Eric gained control of his mount and looked down into the elfin face of a little girl.

"Hope!" Mary was sorry she'd been so strict with the child and had decided to make amends. "Come out here and we'll have some milk and cookies." She waited. "Hope?"

Still no answer. Mary crossed the small living room and opened the door to her daughter's room. "Now Hope, don't sulk. We'll go up presently and see that Mr. O'Malley's been properly cared for. In the meantime…" She peered around the corner and into the cozy bedroom. "Hope?"

Jerking open the bathroom door and checking all the other rooms in the compact cottage took only a few additional seconds. The final fact that convinced Mary of Hope's absence was that the child's coat was missing.

Wide-eyed, Mary ran to the front door, threw it open and peered into the mist. Even on a clear day a person couldn't see all the way to the big house because of the slope of the land but at least most of the pasture was usually visible. Today, that was not the case. Wherever Hope was, she was hidden by the fine curtain of rain.

She'd gone back to see to Mr. O'Malley, of course. That horse meant more to Hope than any threat of punishment for disobeying ever would. Mary recognized that her own judgment had been clouded by the news of Eric's arrival. Had she been thinking clearly, she would have realized how important the horse's welfare was to Hope. What she should have done was take Mr. O'Malley home to their cottage, stable him out back in the small lean-to and let the child finish cooling him down properly, as she'd been taught.

Well, it was too late now. Or was it? Quickly, Mary grabbed a heather-colored woolen scarf, settling it over her head as she dashed out the door. If she could catch Hope before she got as far as the barns, there was a good chance Eric would never see her, never have a chance to figure out the truth.

Mary had agreed to come to Ireland to hide the fact of Hope's birth and hide it she would. All she had to do was be lucky enough to head off her daughter before their whole, happy world collapsed.

"And this is Mr. O'Malley," Hope said proudly. "You can help me brush him if you want." She'd let Eric ferry her back to the barn as soon as she'd gotten over the surprise of seeing a stranger mounted on Caledon.

He smiled down at her as she tugged determinedly on his hand. "This is one of Caledon's sons, you say?"

"Uh-huh. Isn't he wonderful?" The big gelding lowered his head for a hug, his velvety brown nose tucked against Hope's chest, and blew a soft, gentle nicker. She obliged him with a squeeze, then backed off, ruffling his forelock.

Eric glanced toward the place where William stood glaring at him and holding Mr. O'Malley's sire. Both horses were good-looking, but Mr. O'Malley had a gentleness in his eyes that was less noticeable in the stud's gaze. Eric's lips lifted in a wider smile. Perhaps all Caledon needed was the love of such an exceptional child.

"You should see him jump!" Hope said.

Suddenly, Eric tensed, realizing that here beside him stood the daredevil he'd worried about since seeing her sail over the pasture fences. He dropped to one knee and took both her hands in his. "You rode him this morning, didn't you?"

"Yes."

He hesitated. The girl was every bit as fearless speaking to a literal stranger as she had been astride the horse. She had to be the one. "And you took the double jump across the lane, too."

"Oh, no. I'm not allowed to jump the boreen."

"Allowed or not, you did it. I saw you." Troubled, Eric held more tightly to her small fingers. "Don't you know how dangerous it is to do something like that? Haven't your parents taught you anything?"

Hope brightened. "My mother is always tellin' me not to do it," she confessed. "But the poor horse wants to so much and sometimes . . ."

"You can't help yourself," Eric supplied. In the child's hazel eyes he saw an instant spark of rapport.

"Uh-huh! Like when you rode Caledon."

"I'd been asked not to jump him and I didn't," he countered. "That was my responsibility, both to the horse and to Mr. Day."

"But you wanted to. I'll bet that's what you were thinkin' about when you almost ran over me."

Chagrined, Eric nodded. "You may be right." Getting to his feet, he released his hold and was gratified when Hope continued to grasp one of his hands while they strolled in front of the row of stalls. "I wanted to run him full-out."

"I knew it!"

He laughed understandingly. "I'll just bet you did."

Mary stood gathering her courage and catching her breath at the edge of the paddock. The usual pungent smells and sounds of the farm assailed her, yet above all the noise that the horses and grooms were making, she could hear the familiar timbre of one voice she thought she'd managed to forget. The sound of Eric's words, the way he laughed, the warmth of his expressions all came rushing back to overwhelm her. Goose bumps prickled her arms as she lost herself momentarily and silently mouthed his name.

"You're a damn fool, Mary Mulraney," she muttered, disgusted with her initial reactions. "For all he cares, you could be dead and gone." And might as well be, as far as her career was concerned, she added, knowing the thought would help harden her heart all the more. She meant it to. When Eric had rejected her, the absence of his love had left a desperate emptiness in her soul. As soon as she'd discovered she could fill that void with blistering anger and ease the pain, she'd fallen into the habit of using her rage as an elixir. It might not cure anything, but it sure made her feel better.

Mary listened. Hope and Eric were close and getting closer. Her heart raced. Placing her fingertips on her temples she felt the wild beating of her pulse, sensed the in-born call to flee while she still could. She held her breath. The voices were just around the corner.

"You'll like my mother," Hope was saying. "She's very pretty."

"Oh, she is, is she?"

That was Eric! Oh, God. It wasn't a bad dream! Mary's fists clenched. Run, her mind commanded. He'll never know. You don't have to see him again.

But that wasn't true. Hope was with him. Her darling Hope. If the wrong things were said or if Eric learned the child was a Mulraney and began to ask embarrassing questions, what then?

Hope's clear, sweet voice was carried on the still air. "Uncle John says my mother is the best rider in the whole world."

"Mr. Day is your uncle? I figured he was your father."

She momentarily hung her head. "I don't have a real father."

"I see."

Bravely, before she could change her mind, Mary took a deep breath and stepped around the corner to solidly block their path.

"No, you don't see, Mr. Lambert," she announced in a clear, strong voice. "Hope is *my* daughter."

Chapter Three

Breaking away from Eric, Hope skipped over to her mother, grasped her hand and began tugging her closer to the man who waited, his mouth agape.

"This is the man Uncle John wanted to show Caledon to, Mama. He's famous."

"I know, dear," Mary said calmly, her words a hollow echo of the intense emotions coursing through her. Eric looked almost the same but not quite. He was still tall, athletic-looking and slim, with a square chin, emerald-green eyes and thick, wavy dark hair, yet he was also more masculine somehow. Devastatingly so. The excitement reflected in his expression took her breath away!

Mary nodded to him and spoke nonchalantly, as if his presence meant little to her. "How are you, Eric?"

"Mary? Mary Mulraney? Is that really you?" Breaking into a smile, he took a step toward her.

Mary gave ground, her nostrils flaring, her eyes and body language telegraphing hostility. "I'm surprised you know my name."

Puzzled, he halted. His grin faded. "Of course I know your name. Where have you been? What happened to you?"

"Nothing that would interest you, I'm sure." Turning to Hope, Mary gave her a stern look. "You, young lady, are in serious trouble."

"I cleaned up my room," Hope countered.

"Then came back here when I told you not to."

"But—"

"No buts. Get on up to the house and help your aunt Katie in the kitchen. And you mind me this time, or else. You hear?"

"Yes." Hope's smile was tentative and directed at Eric. "She's usually nicer than this, Mr. Lambert. She's just a little mad at me right now."

"And she doesn't know the half of it," he replied.

"You won't tell…" Holding her breath, the naughty child waited.

"No, I probably won't," he hedged, "if you *swear* you won't do it again."

She crossed her heart dramatically. "I swear."

Mary scowled at them both. "Do what?"

"Nothing," Eric said firmly.

Concentrating on Hope, Mary continued to press for an explanation. "What happened?" She waited. No answer was forthcoming. "I assume you were jumping again?"

Hope hung her head and nodded. "Yes, ma'am."

"That figures. Well, we'll discuss all that later, when we're alone. For now, to the house. March," Mary ordered, pointing. "And no detours. I'll finish brushing down Mr. O'Malley."

Off at a run, Hope quickly reached the gray stone manor and disappeared inside. It wasn't until then that Mary looked back at Eric. The tumultuous storms of an Irish winter were bland compared to what she was feeling at the moment.

Eric's mood had begun to mimic hers. "Now, are you ready to tell me what in blazes is wrong with you?"

"Nothing is wrong with me. I'm the same person I always was." Lifting one eyebrow, she added, "I'll thank you not to mention to anyone else that we ever met before today."

"Fine." He scowled. "Like hell you're the same. The Mary Mulraney I remember was at least civil."

"I'm being civil. I didn't have you thrown off the place, did I?"

Eric's laugh was humorless. "I doubt you'd be able to do that even if you wanted to. I'm here on business."

"So Uncle John said." Picking up a brush, she slipped her hand through the strap on the back and entered Mr. O'Malley's stall. To her consternation, Eric followed and took up a position on the opposite side of the horse.

"And the girl?" he asked.

"My daughter. I suppose she told you her name was Hope Mulraney?"

"We hadn't gotten around to formal introductions. When she saw me up on Caledon she accepted me as an old friend."

"I see."

"No, I don't think you do see. An attitude like that can be dangerous."

"Don't be silly."

"At the very least, she should be taught never to approach strangers so trustingly. Not everyone is as safe as I am."

Mary's anger flared. Hope was safe with Eric, all right, but she knew from the pounding of her heart that she wasn't. That, however, was the last thing she wanted him to guess. Continuing to brush the horse's flanks, she made a sour face at him.

"All right. Have it your way," he said with resignation. "I can see you're mad at me, but that doesn't change the facts. Your little girl is getting seriously out of control, and even if you can't see it, I can."

Too upset with Eric and with herself to think clearly, Mary vented her thoughts before censoring them. "And what makes *you* such an expert, Mr. Lambert? Are you a father?"

The careless taunt stuck in her throat and she glanced away quickly, hoping the guilt in her remark had not registered with him. She chanced a surreptitious peek. Little showed in his expression except questions and what she supposed were bruised feelings. Well, too bad. It wasn't her fault. She hadn't invited him to Ireland.

"I don't have to be a father to recognize a volatile situation," he said, deciding Mary was not going to listen unless he gave her solid reasons to take him seriously. "I saw your daughter take some difficult jumps today—a bounce and combination, for starters. You're damn lucky she didn't fall."

Mary humphed and continued brushing the horse, her vigor fueled by her temper. "She told me she was jumping. I'll take care of it." When Eric stopped arguing and stepped back to lean against the wall of the stall, his arms folded across his chest, she realized she'd seen that determined look on his face before. If he had his way, their heated conversation wasn't over. "Go away, Eric."

"I'm a guest here."

"Then go on up to the house. Leave me alone."

His reply was less irate than it was sorrowful. "Why, Mary?" He circled Mr. O'Malley and stopped a few feet from her. "Is it because of what happened at the '84 Olympics?"

"I don't know what you're talking about."

"That's it, isn't it?" Lightly taking her arm, he stilled it and stopped her from stepping away.

She shrugged off his touch with more vigor than was necessary. "Forget it, Eric. I have. Just do what you did then and kiss me off. It should be easy for you. You've had enough practice."

"Oh, for the love of—"

"*Love* had nothing to do with it. You made that fact crystal clear. Now, go away." The unyielding look in Eric's eyes shook Mary's resolve but she remained stiffly demanding.

"I don't think I should, just yet," he said, his slow, sensuous drawl reminiscent of nothing Mary had ever heard from him before. She saw then that she'd miscalculated, given Eric too little credit for having become a mature, forceful man. The boy she had loved and lost was gone. The man she now confronted would no longer do her bidding simply because she lifted her chin and stubbornly insisted.

Eric began to smile, his hand raising to recapture her arm. He guided her out of the stall and stepped clear to let the door swing shut. Taking the brush from her hand, he tossed it aside, then followed it with the cap John had loaned him.

Slowly, he drew the scarf from Mary's head, freeing her curls, and took a damp strand in his fingers, rubbing it as if he'd never seen or touched anything so fine before. In the next instant, she was crushed to his chest.

Mary struggled against him until she realized that the more she resisted, the more tightly he held her. "What do you think you're doing?"

"Just what you told me to," he replied, brushing his lips across her forehead and down her temples.

"I never told you anything of the kind, Eric Lambert, and you know it."

"You said to kiss you the way I did in '84 and I'm trying to oblige."

She turned her head away and ducked against the coarse wool of his jacket. He smelled of heather and wool and he reminded her of the warm Irish springtime. Mustering her ire, she looked up at him. "Not kissed me—kissed me off. Didn't want anything more to do with me. If you recall, you insisted you were sorry."

Silently, she cursed the tears that threatened to spill onto her cheeks. To be this close to Eric again was not as she remembered it; it was a thousand times better, a thousand times worse. The last time he'd held her they'd been little more than children. Eric wasn't the only one who'd matured, and Mary's traitorous woman's body was responding to him in spite of her resolve to resist. It mattered little that her reactions didn't show. She knew they were there and that was enough to jolt her. Plenty.

Releasing his hold, Eric cupped her cheeks in his hands and held her face so she couldn't turn away again. "Was I really so harsh, Mary? I remember it differently. It was early in the morning and I didn't know what to say to you. We'd been pretty good friends, up till then. I thought I should apologize for losing control. That was all I meant."

"No." Mary's voice trembled, her fists coming to rest against Eric's chest.

"Yes. I'm sure I only wanted to comfort you. I figured I'd already hurt you enough with my adolescent behavior."

An escaping tear trickled down Mary's cheek and he caught it with his thumb, brushing it away as he went on. "I wonder why I never realized how beautiful you are, Mary

Mulraney, with your sky-blue eyes, copper-colored hair and your Irish temper. I was a fool not to take you more seriously when I had the chance, wasn't I?'' She twisted, trying to get away, but he held her fast. ''Well, it's true. And now that I've found you again, I'm at least going to try to see to it that you've truly forgiven me. We were friends once. We shouldn't be enemies now.'' Sighing, he lowered his mouth and claimed hers.

Mary caught her breath. Nothing in any of her dreams or memories had prepared her for the current potency of Eric's kiss. The muscles of her body tensed, but no longer in preparation for escape. Unmindful of where she was or who might be watching, she drew her arms around his neck and pressed herself to him.

His response was as expected. Groaning, he pulled her closer and deepened the kiss, claiming not only her lips but her soul, as well. Mary parted her lips, her tongue meeting his, the taste a sweet remembrance. In that instant, she could have been eighteen again. Happy. Free. Desperately in love.

Reality crashed in on her like the hard, unforgiving ground rising up during a fall from a galloping horse. She wasn't eighteen. Nor was she free. There was Hope to consider. Hope, who was a joyful, well-adjusted child without a care in the world. Hope, whose life had brought Mary the only true happiness and love she'd ever known. Nothing must ever spoil that. Nothing!

She pushed Eric away with such abruptness this time that he easily let her go. Puzzled at the sudden change in her attitude, he reached out a hand to her. ''Mary?''

''No. Leave me alone. I told you already. I don't want to go back to the way I was, the life I lived. I'm happy here.'' To give her hands something to do, she tugged down the hem of her heavy sweater.

''Why are you so afraid?''

"Don't be silly."

Pensive, Eric stepped back. "All right. If you're not scared of me, then what's the problem?"

"I told you. I just want to be left alone."

"With your daughter?"

"With my daughter. Go back to the States and stop bothering me."

"Why are you so adamant?"

"I'm just being sensible." Whatever she did, Mary knew she had to keep him from asking too many direct questions about Hope. "Look. It's simple. I loved someone once, and I'm cured for life, that's all. I refuse to get involved with anyone again."

"Hope's father?"

The question was put so gently Mary's heart wrenched. "Yes."

"I am sorry. But surely you and I can still be friends."

"There's no point. You have your life and I have mine. After today, we'll probably never see each other again." The words nearly stuck in her throat.

A slight smile lifted the corners of Eric's mouth. "I wouldn't be too sure of that. Your uncle has invited me to spend a few nights here to discuss a business deal and I've accepted his kind offer. I'm sure we'll be seeing plenty of each other."

"That's impossible!"

He chuckled. "Not at all. I'll admit I was a little surprised when he telephoned, but—"

"*He* telephoned? Coming here wasn't your idea?"

"As a matter of fact, no. I'd seen Caledon work, in his prime, of course, and John and I had casually discussed the differences and similarities in our breeding programs when we met a few times on the circuit, but that was all."

"Go on." Mary's uneasiness increased.

"He told me he was watching the Open Jumping from Madison Square Garden on television a few weeks ago, saw my horse stumble, and began to remember our earlier contacts. He said he figured I could use a replacement soon and also wanted his stock bred to advantage. So, he got in touch with me and here I am."

Mary's mind was whirling. Of all the stupid coincidences. Why couldn't her uncle have chosen some other world-class rider to befriend? Why did it have to be Eric? What were the odds against a random choice like that, anyway? If she hadn't been so certain the secret of Hope's parentage had been kept from John and Katie since the outset, she might have given in to the panic nibbling away at her nerves.

Squaring her shoulders, she stared boldly at Eric. "So, you figured, while you were here, you'd give good old Mary the thrill of her life and romance her, did you?" The grin on his face spread and Mary wondered just how furious she could get before exploding from the pressure.

"The idea did occur to me a couple of minutes ago."

Hands on hips, she glared up at him. "Of course it did. You're Eric Lambert, the dashing champion with a trail of broken hearts that stretches around the globe, aren't you?"

He was laughing now. "I think I may have missed Denmark."

"Oh! For heaven's sake."

Eyeing her tightly clenched fists, Eric shook his head. "And I thought the tales of Irish tempers were nothing more than fairy stories." A man's whistle coming from behind him made him start and whirl around.

Mary's cheeks grew flushed. "William! How long have you been there?"

"A while," the groom said. Ignoring Mary, he smiled at Eric. "You don't want to be pushin' her too far, I'll be thinkin'." He handed the younger man the cap he'd tossed aside earlier. "She may have been born and raised in California but her soul is pure Ireland."

Accepting the hat and dusting it off before putting it on, Eric nodded. "I'm glad to see your cough is better, sir. Must have been something you had stuck in your throat."

"That it was," William said, beginning to grin in his typically crooked sort of way. "It'll take a few pints of Guinness to clear it, for certain. Would you like to be joinin' me?"

"William!" Mary stared at the two men, willing them to be enemies for her sake. It didn't work.

"I'd be delighted," Eric said. "The air's getting a bit thick around here."

"Likely to blow up a storm," the groom added. "You'd best come with me for safety."

As Mary watched them sauntering away, it was all she could do to keep from screaming her anger and frustration to the world. Safety, indeed! Men, especially some of the Irishmen she'd met, seemed to hold the distorted view that women were okay in their proper places, yet still took looking after, like a flock of dumb sheep. The last thing she wanted at this point in her life was to have Eric Lambert picking up that kind of archaic idea from Will or John. His own notions were obviously bad enough.

Behind her, Mr. O'Malley nickered softly, tossed his head and blew a puff of air at her.

"And what are *you* laughing at?" she grumbled. Scooping up her scarf, she spun around and stomped off through the puddles in the paddock. This promised to be a harrowing evening, and she had no doubt it was only the beginning.

They cut across the fields and climbed a stile to reach the road. Walking along beside William, Eric shook his head as he mulled over Mary's strange behavior. Beyond that, he also wondered why he'd felt the need to antagonize her when it looked as if she was already so mad at him she was barely rational.

He supposed it all went back to the days when they'd competed. Mary's mood was often sad, but he'd usually been able to raise her spirits with good-natured teasing. The trouble was, he hadn't suspected she had such a crush on him.

He looked over at William. "How long have you known Mary?"

The old man cleared his throat and scuffed at a pebble on the road before speaking. "Since she came to Ireland."

"And when was that?"

"Before the girl was born."

"Hope." Eric pondered his affinity for the child. "She's quite a rider."

"Comes by it naturally," Will said, "with a mother like Mary."

"I suppose that's true, up to a point. What kind of schooling has she had?"

"You mean for her riding?"

"Yes." Eric stuffed his cold hands into the pockets of his jacket.

"None, except what I've taught her and what her mother's thought she needed to know to be safe." He paused and laid his hand on Eric's arm. "You thinkin' of teachin' her?"

"Me? No. She needs a full-time coach and a lot more discipline in her life than I could give her in the short time I'll be here." Beginning to smile, he nodded at the older man. "I can see you're concerned. So am I. It's just that I'm not in any position to help." He snorted disgustedly. "Hell, Mary doesn't even *like* me, let alone want me to coach her daughter, even if I could."

"You teach in the States?" Will asked, continuing their walk.

"Not all the time. I'm affiliated with a bunch of other ex-Olympians and eventers who choose the students they feel have the most potential. When I'm home, I judge their progress. Why?"

The old man shrugged. "Just wonderin'. How many mares do you have?"

"If I didn't know better, I'd swear I was standing here talking to John Day. He asked me the same questions." Studying the expression of innocence on Will's face, Eric replied, glad to have a reason to swing his disturbing thoughts away from Mary and Hope. "Seven mares, three geldings, not counting Dutchman's Pride, who's ready to retire, and no stallions. But in these days of modern artificial breeding, I hardly need one, now do I?"

With a chuckle, the shorter man drew his fingers along the gray stubble on his chin. "Sort of takes the fun out of it, though, doesn't it? Poor old Caledon has sons and daughters all over the world and doesn't even know it. Seems a shame."

They reached a village that was so small it had only three businesses, as far as Eric could tell. One of the stone buildings sported a hanging sign with a picture of a brimming mug of ale and the word O'Malley's. He cocked his head at Will. "The horse's namesake?"

"The same. He lives upstairs but he spends a lot of his free time at Day's."

Leading the way inside, Will introduced Eric by making an announcement to everyone at once, then approached the highly polished oak bar where a tall, burly man in an apron waited, grinning.

"And this is O'Malley. Give my friend Eric, here, a smilin' pint and the same for me, if you will." In a grandiose gesture he slapped a handful of coins on the bar.

Eric was still trying to get his eyes to adjust to the dim light when O'Malley slid an enormous mug of ale in front of him. Etched in the thick foam on the top was a face with a grin.

"To Mary Mulraney," Will said, hoisting his mug and holding it out. O'Malley, too, lifted a glass.

Eric joined in the toast. "To Mary." He'd taken a tentative sip of the strong brew and was trying to think of a polite way to keep from having to down it all when O'Malley added, "And how is my darlin' Mary?"

Eric's throat constricted in the middle of a swallow. Choking and coughing, he pushed his mug aside and tried not to blow foam from his ale all over the bar and his companions.

Will was thumping him on the back. "Not used to our Irish brew, are ye, son?"

"No...I guess not," Eric managed between wheezes. "Sorry. I appreciate your generosity but I'm not much of a drinker, as a rule."

"No matter. If you're plannin' on havin' dinner with Mr. John, you'd best be startin' back, anyway. I'll do you the honor of polishin' off your pint."

Eric got to his feet and nodded politely to the bartender before addressing his companion. "Thanks. The next time's on me. Walk me to the door, Will?"

"Sure." The old man chugalugged the remainder of his ale, wiped his mouth with the back of his hand and followed Eric outside.

"Is O'Malley Hope's father?" Eric asked, surprised to feel his gut tie in a hard knot as he voiced the question. The man was young enough to be and not all that bad-looking, if one liked the overmuscled, hulking type. Did Mary? Might she have given herself to the amiable man behind the bar?

"O'Malley?" Will chuckled and lifted his eyebrows higher. "Why do you ask?"

"I just wondered."

"Can't say," Will drawled.

"Can't? Or won't?"

Will started back into the pub, then paused. "I do know O'Malley would marry the lass in a minute if she'd say the word." He smiled and winked at Eric. "Many's the child been raised in a pub and none the worse for it. You'd best go. The family eats at five, on the dot."

Eric thanked him again, turned on his heel and started up the road at a trot. Marriage? To the pub owner? Mary must realize she'd never be happy without her daily, unhampered contact with horses. Neither would Hope. The thought of the two of them living above the bar, away from their beloved sport, rankled him. He frowned. Surely Mary wouldn't be foolish enough to marry simply to give Hope a flesh-and-blood father. Or would she?

He quickened his pace. He was the one who'd insisted she wasn't doing a good enough job raising Hope alone. Now he prayed he hadn't inadvertently pushed her closer to a decision that would be a terrible mistake for all concerned.

Eric's jaw and fists clenched. How in the hell had he gotten so damned involved in Mary's current life in so short a time, anyway? And why should he care? Guilt? No. They'd known each other fairly well for two or three seasons, but there'd been almost four years' difference in their ages and they really hadn't spent a lot of social time together. God knows, he hadn't meant to make love to her. Hell, she was just a kid.

They hadn't seen each other for years, and truth be told, except for occasionally remembering his own embarrassment and Mary's tears on the morning after, he hadn't thought of her very often once she'd left the circuit. Besides, what possible difference could he make when he lived half a world away? Why even try?

Ignoring the stile, Eric vaulted over the fence and strode across the sloping pasture. Damp grass wet his boots and the mist made his thick, dark hair curl even more than usual. He ran his fingers through it and pushed it back. Damned if he knew what was wrong with him, but something sure was. The feelings in the pit of his stomach were the same as if he'd just cleared a difficult jump and then seen that the next hurdle was impossible.

Chapter Four

To refuse to dine at her uncle's table when she had almost always done so would have caused far too much interest in her reasons, so Mary subdued her pride, ignored her nervousness as best she could, and went, mumbling to herself all the way.

Coming up the path to the main house, she remembered seeing it for the first time. The exterior had looked as cold and forbidding as it still did, yet how warm and friendly the living quarters had actually been with their leftover nineteenth-century furnishings and gilt-framed portraits of generations of splendid horses. Mary knew that she had arrived in Ireland terribly hurt and upset at her own parents' attitudes and she had unknowingly transferred that animosity to her aunt and uncle before actually getting to know them. That was why she'd turned down their invitation to live with them in the big house.

She smiled to herself. Everything had worked out for the best, though. The cottage she'd chosen was her favorite

place to be, other than astride a good horse. If she'd re-
sided with Katie and John from the beginning, moving out
later without hurting their feelings would have been impossible. She'd never purposely cause them grief, which was one
reason why she'd continued to masquerade as a widow even
after growing to love her extended family. They were kind
beyond measure. Hearing of her need and taking her in on
the strength of blood relationship alone, they'd accepted
her, and later Hope, without question. She wanted desperately to keep it that way.

The days of butlers and maids at the old stone manor
house were long past, so Mary wiped her boots on the mat
on the porch, nudged a nosy cat aside and let herself in the
kitchen door. Katie, who often reminded everyone she was
plump only because she was the clan's official food taster,
stood at the stove, stirring the contents of an iron kettle.
From the familiar aroma, Mary knew it was vegetable soup.

"That smells heavenly." She gave the older woman a kiss
on the cheek and took the spoon from her. "I'd better make
sure it's as good as usual, though." Lifting the ladle, she
sipped. "Mmm. You're hired."

"That's what John said years ago. Look what it got me."

Laughing, Mary glanced around the large, warm kitchen.
"Where's Hope? I sent her up here to help you and she
never came home to get cleaned up for dinner."

"In the other room . . . with John and our guest."

Mary pulled a face, her heart beginning to beat faster. "I
should have known."

"You look lovely tonight," Katie told her. "I've not seen
that particular sweater since the last festival at Meath. I
thought you were saving it."

The knowing smile spreading across her aunt's face made
Mary blush. She ran her damp palms over her jeans, osten-

sibly to smooth the denim. "I'm behind in my laundry. This was all I had that was clean."

"Ah. I see." Pushing her short, salt-and-pepper hair off her forehead with the back of her wrist, Katie gestured toward the heavily laden kitchen table. "You can begin carrying in the food for me, if you will."

Mary obliged. The table in the long dining room was spread with Katie's finest linen, Waterford crystal and china, as was always the case when John entertained buyers. But tonight the whole room seemed brighter, more cheerful. Her aunt had arranged pink-and-yellow roses as a centerpiece and the effect was most pleasing. She placed the bread and potatoes and went back for the platter of roast.

"Your roses have scented the whole room," Mary said. "You should use them like that more often."

Katie lifted a brimming soup tureen, balancing it carefully as she led the way back to the dining table. "It was John's idea. Surprised the bejabbers out of me, I'll tell you." Pausing briefly to survey her handiwork and adjust a napkin, she called out to her husband and smiled as he ushered Eric into the room.

"You know Eric Lambert, don't you, Mary?" John said in the booming voice that was his trademark.

"We met at the stables this afternoon." More uptight than she'd thought, she tugged at the hem of her teal-blue sweater to give her hands something to do besides flutter aimlessly.

"You look just like summer itself," John observed. He cocked his balding head at Eric. "That outfit really makes her eyes look like the sky, doesn't it?"

"An Irish sky," Eric replied, smiling slightly. "Just a bit stormy."

Mary glared at him. The black turtleneck he wore under his jacket reminded her of the time they'd both competed in

Calgary, Alberta. The rest of his clothing also fit his athlete's body all too well. Hope was not only at his side, she was tugging on the sleeve of his tweed jacket.

"What do *my* eyes look like?" the child demanded. "Sky, too?"

Leaning over to be more on her level, Eric placed his hands on his knees and studied her upturned face. "Maybe the freshest spring grass," he ventured. When she looked unhappy about his description, he added, "It's the very best and sweetest of the year, just like you."

Satisfied, Hope grinned at her mother. "Can I sit by Eric, Mama?"

"You have your regular place," she said flatly, taking care to try to sound normal when she was feeling anything but.

John spoke up. "Ah, Mary, let the child sit where she wants. For too long she's had nobody but me and Will to fuss over her."

Jerking her chair out and sitting down hard, Mary gritted her teeth and took deep breaths intended to induce calm while she reminded herself that the placement of a chair at the dinner table was not worth getting upset over. Unfortunately, her efforts had little beneficial effect.

"You and Will Murphy have spoiled her plenty already," she said. The hard edge to her voice made her cringe inwardly. Her aunt and uncle didn't deserve her ire. If she didn't get better control of herself soon, everyone was sure to notice. Since the only change in her life was Eric's arrival, it wouldn't be hard to guess the cause of her disquiet if they gave it some thought.

Her uncle's warm laugh filled the room. "True, true. But she and you are all the children Katie and I have ever had. Give us a break, as you used to say."

Everyone at the table was smiling, except Mary, and seemed to be waiting for her reply. "All right, all of you give me a break, too," she insisted, tongue in cheek, trying her best to convince her subconscious that it was safe to join in the mood of celebration. The jesting did make her feel better.

Pouring wine for everyone but Hope, John raised his glass. "Here's to good friends well met..." Mary began to sip her wine. When her uncle added, "and a promising partnership," she thought she'd strangle.

Wide-eyed, she looked from her uncle to Eric and back again and sputtered, "A *what?*"

"A business deal." Putting down his glass, John began dishing up soup for Hope before passing the tureen to his guests. "We've been discussing placing some of the Day horses in the States to be crossed with the Thoroughbreds and Warmbloods Eric has."

"You wouldn't." She stared, her fingers gripping the edge of the table.

Eric's smile was pleasant even though it didn't light his eyes. He finished ladling soup and passed the tureen as if he had taken no special note of her strong reaction. "We're still discussing the finer points, Ms. Mulraney. I suggest you give all of us one of your famous breaks."

"But...these young horses need the grass on The Curragh to develop good bone. Everyone knows that."

"Kentucky has similar growing conditions. So do other parts of the world. They may not be as well known, but with proper care and supplementation if necessary, equally good results can be achieved." Lifting his soup spoon, Eric began to eat. So did everyone else, except Mary.

"I don't believe this." Flabbergasted, she sank back into her chair. "Uncle John, why would you consider such a thing? You're doing fine here. You always have."

He nodded, lay his spoon aside and blotted his lips with his napkin. "But I can do better. That's the whole point of breeding fine animals in the first place—improvement of the lines. If each generation isn't better than the one before, I've made no gains." Smiling at Hope, he went on. "Besides, our little leprechaun here needs what Eric can offer, too."

Mary's heart stopped for a long moment, then began to crash against the walls of her chest, beating wildly. When John had tied Hope's name to Eric's, she'd felt her world spinning off its axis. "What do you mean?"

"I've approached him about arranging some serious lessons for her and he's agreed," John said.

Hope's squeal of delight was so loud the tabby cat lounging in a quiet corner of the room jumped up and ran out.

Something inside Mary snapped. No longer could she keep up the pretense that everything was fine. It was *not* fine. Not by a long shot. She could not—would not—permit this farce to continue.

"No." Springing to her feet, she stared at Eric, willing him to decline. "I'm her mother and I say no lessons."

Calmly, slowly, Eric spoke. "It's not definite. Nothing is. We're merely discussing possibilities." His voice deepened. "I didn't think you'd be so against it."

Hope's shrill, continuous protest was grating on Mary's nerves. Everyone at the table seemed to be babbling at her at once. Her nostrils flared as she looked at each of them in turn. "Stop it! All of you." The gaggle subsided.

Katie reached out to touch Mary's arm. "Please, dear. Sit down. Let's finish eating before we discuss any more business."

"This is not business we're discussing, it's my daughter," Mary protested, lowering herself cautiously into her chair. "I've told you all, over and over, I don't want her riding in competitions. Ever. And that's final. End of discussion."

"We understand how you feel," her aunt assured her. "And we don't mean to gang up on you, but everyone knows she's been jumping Mr. O'Malley on her own. Better she learns proper, safe techniques from an expert. At least consider it."

Mary had considered it. Plenty. Trembling, she clenched her hands in her lap to keep her frustration and anger from showing more than they already did and addressed her uncle. "If and when I think formal lessons are necessary, *I'll* teach her." One glance at Eric told her he was listening intently. His comment followed swiftly.

"It's probably been a long time since you've competed."

"I work my uncle's horses every day," Mary countered. "No one has complained."

"Training horses and coaching people is not the same skill, although you need knowledge of both to succeed. I've been involved in teaching for the past five years. In a year or so I plan to retire from competition and concentrate more fully on instructing and traveling with my students. I expect it to be very rewarding."

Mary's fists clenched. "Forget it. I'd never let Hope leave Ireland, anyway."

"Whatever you say." Eric leaned forward across the table to concentrate on Mary. "However, if your uncle and I can come to terms on specific points, she wouldn't have to. I'll be visiting over here a few months of every year."

Hope's voice rose. "Oh, boy! Me and Mr. O'Malley will be great!"

"I said no," Mary repeated. The tears that began to flow down the child's cheeks were shed quietly, without ballyhoo, yet had the same effect on Mary's tender heart as if she were sobbing inconsolably.

"Would you care to tell us precisely why?" Eric asked.

"Gladly. Competition takes all the fun out of riding, for one thing, and pushes a horse and rider too far and into too much unnecessary risk-taking. And that's just for starters. Believe me, I know. Hope doesn't have to train with an expert or travel all over the world like some compulsive nomad to have a good time, and that's what really matters." Gathering up her napkin, Mary plopped it down beside her plate and got to her feet. "Now, if you'll all excuse me, I've lost my appetite."

She paused in silent contemplation of her daughter. Tears still streaked Hope's rosy cheeks and her nose was running, but she was doing a surprisingly adult job of controlling her emotions. Keeping the child from riding for simple pleasure had never been Mary's goal. Keeping her from Eric, however, was imperative.

Speaking loudly and firmly, Mary reinforced her decision. "If the time comes that I think Hope is ready to be taught the finer points of competitive riding, I will be the one to teach her." Nodding to Eric, then the others, she turned and left the room.

Puzzled, Eric shook his head and tried to concentrate on his meal. He'd never really noticed prior examples of the stubborn, feisty streak Mary had just displayed. As a girl, she'd bowed to her parents' wishes so easily that her current actions seemed out of character. At that moment, he'd have given just about anything to learn what had changed her so dramatically, what had made her such a different person from the one he thought he knew.

Penitent, Mary returned later to help Katie clear the table and make sure Hope understood she was to stay and help. Then, Mary hurried to the stables, chose two of John's best geldings, had them saddled and took them to the base of the granite steps leading out of the house. It was her uncle's habit to walk through his stables every evening and she knew he'd include Eric in his after-dinner jaunt. Tonight, she'd be waiting with a plan of her own when they appeared.

Leading the way out the heavy mahogany front door, Eric saw her and stopped. So did John.

Mary swallowed hard and managed to muster a smile. "I want to apologize."

Without expression, Eric nodded.

"Accepted," John said. He eyed the horses whose reins she held. "You planning on riding two at once?"

"I thought maybe Mr. Lambert would like to see our cross-country training area."

John smiled. "A fine idea. But if you meant that other horse for me, I'll have to decline." He patted his still-firm stomach. "Too much of Katie's lemon pie."

"I meant the horse for myself," Mary said boldly. "I can show him around." Climbing up onto the stone stoop at the foot of the balustrade the same way Hope often did, she stepped lightly aboard the first horse without assistance and leaned down to fit her feet into the stirrup irons.

Still silent, Eric approached the other horse, adjusted the length of the stirrup leathers, checked the girth straps, then vaulted effortlessly into the saddle. Two crash helmets were strung together by their chin straps and draped over the neck of Mary's mount, just in front of the saddle.

She handed one of them to him. "Here. Put this on."

He complied and watched as she did the same.

"I still hate the feel of these," she remarked. "But I try to set a good example for Hope. I keep telling myself they're no more cumbersome or heavy than a cap."

"They aren't."

"I know." Mary adjusted the chin strap while John held her horse's bridle. "I do miss the feel of the wind blowing through my hair, though."

The sudden tightening of his gut surprised Eric. That was the way he'd always pictured Mary, with her horse running full-out and the California sun glistening off her beautiful hair. It came to him then: that was what had tugged at his memory when he'd first glimpsed Hope. She had Mary's hair.

Reining her horse to the right, Mary led the way out of the yard and down the lane at a walk to warm up the horses slowly. Eric followed, his thoughts random, yet still focused on the little girl. She was a precocious child, old beyond her years, no doubt due to her constant adult companionship. She had Mary's long, pretty eyelashes, too, and those eyes... Mary's were blue, while Hope's were a sort of emerald-tinged hazel. Like his. Just like his.

The thought quickened his pulse the same way the start of a cross-country race always did and he pressed his heels into his horse's flanks in order to draw up beside Mary.

She turned to look over at him, then lowered her eyes. "I really am sorry I behaved so badly at dinner."

"It's forgotten."

"I would like to be friends. Like the old days."

He studied her. "All right. We can try."

"As your friend, I'd like to ask a favor," she began, hoping she sounded sincere, not as manipulative as she felt.

"Ask." Eric watched her wet her lips, saw how carefully she was proceeding. The same determination he'd noticed at dinner still lurked in her eyes, only now it had apprehension and guile to keep it company.

"I'd like you to voluntarily promise to stay away from Hope. She's young and impressionable and I don't want her deciding she wants to compete just because you've awed her with your fame or success or tales of your trophies.''

Waiting to see what else she might say, Eric rode along in silence for lengthy moments. When he finally did speak, it was to ask, ''Exactly how old is Hope, Mary?''

Her head snapped up, her nostrils flaring. ''What possible difference can that make?''

''None...if she didn't have green eyes.'' Eric felt his posture stiffen. ''So, tell me. How old is she and who is her father?''

Mary pressed her knees tight to the gelding's withers, leaned forward and kicked him into a canter. She knew she could never outrun Eric, nor was that her intent. She simply needed time to think, to formulate an answer that would placate him without getting her into worse trouble.

The lane bent right. Cross poles, striped with red and white, were the only gate across the opening in the fence leading to the practice field. She paced her horse to begin the trial run and sensed Eric behind her, doing the same.

Lengthening shadows distorted some of the terrain, but Mary wasn't worried. Both Bounder, Eric's horse, and hers, Pint of Guinness, were well acquainted with the overland course and not likely to balk or miss a hazard. As cautious as Eric always was, she was certain he'd let her remain in the lead. He hadn't walked the course ahead of time to plan his strategy and familiarize himself with each jump and he'd never ridden Bounder before, either, so she could be assured he wouldn't try to pass her.

This time, she was wrong. Close at her left shoulder she felt the hot breath of his mount. Up the bank, down and over the drop on the other side, they raced. Eric pulled ahead, his horse's hooves splashing water high in the air as it vaulted a hedge and galloped through the shallow trench on the far side.

The atmosphere crackled with excitement. Mary leaned into the jumps and concentrated. Her horse was normally the better of the two, but with Eric up on Bounder, the bay had never looked or performed better. She couldn't believe her eyes when he pulled farther and farther ahead.

Cresting a rise, she found Eric leaning forward to pat his horse's neck and waiting for her. Although she could have pressed on by him, she stopped.

"Whew! That was some ride."

"Foolish," he countered. "I know better and so do you."

"These horses have run the course lots of times," she said, still a bit breathless. "I knew they'd do fine."

"But I didn't. And I raced you, anyway, because I was upset." Chagrined, Eric slid to the ground. "We need to talk."

She nodded. Swinging her right leg over the saddle, she prepared to let herself down. Eric took up a position behind her, ready to help.

"I can do it alone," Mary insisted.

"You can do lots of things alone. We all can. That doesn't mean it's the best way." Staying close, he put his hands at her waist and assisted her descent.

Defiant, she spun to face him. The dark look on his face was intimidating, but not enough to dissuade her from speaking out. "That's my affair."

"Is that what it was, Mary? An affair? Did you run off with some lowlife who got you pregnant and then ditched you?" The thought turned his stomach.

"No!"

"Then what? Who? John says you were widowed. Is that right?" He grasped her shoulders. "Tell me."

"I'll do nothing of the kind. It's none of your business."

"Isn't it? Or is it really so much my business that you're afraid to tell me?" The panic-stricken look on her face was his answer. The truth he'd been shoving to the back of his mind and denying forced itself to the fore and a glow of unexpected warmth suffused him. "My God, Mary. She's mine."

"No! Hope is *mine*. Only mine. Can't you understand that?" Desperate, she grasped the lapels of his coat. "Please, Eric. Don't spoil everything."

He jerked away from her. "Spoil it? Me?" Pacing, he whirled to face her. "When I think of all the time that's passed, all the miracles I've missed . . . Why didn't you tell me?"

"Tell you?" Mary's vision blurred with tears. "You didn't want anything to do with me, remember? What was I supposed to do, drop you a postcard and inform you I had a little surprise for you?"

"So, instead, you ran away to Ireland."

"Ran away? Hah! My parents pitched a fit, disowned me and packed me off to Ireland by lying to poor Uncle John. I had my baby, raised her myself and made a good life for us. And that's how it will stay."

"No, it won't," he said solemnly.

Watching Mary's changing expression, he could see her anger and aversion to him building, yet his conscience wouldn't let him back down. He owed a lot more than riding lessons to the lovely little girl he already adored. It wasn't a matter of financial support, although he intended to provide that as well. It was the wildness, the disobedient and dangerous streak he'd repeatedly glimpsed in Hope's actions that made his decision easier. Mary was worried about the child, too, but for the wrong reasons. Somebody had to intercede and Fate had seen to it that he got the job, like it or not.

Facing Mary, Eric stood firm. She was too blind and stubborn to see the situation as clearly as he could. If he did as she asked and walked away, he might be consigning his daughter to the life of an invalid. Or worse. The way the child took chances, it was only a matter of time before the law of averages caught up to her and she paid dearly for her folly. He could never turn his back on her.

"I won't tell her I'm her father," he said. "But I won't get out of her life, either."

"I hate you!" Mary screeched. She tried to pummel him with her fists but he grabbed both wrists and held her off.

"That's your prerogative. You created the lie, and for Hope's sake, I'll keep your secret. However, I suggest you begin to treat me with some respect or it's you she'll be questioning, not me."

Mary continued to struggle. Eric didn't want to squeeze her wrists so tightly that he inadvertently hurt her. Neither could he release her unless he wanted a black eye or broken nose for his trouble. She was breathing hard, her cheeks flushed, her eyes bright with tears, her breasts heaving beneath the soft wool of her sweater. She was awakening a primitive aspect of his personality he didn't like, the male animal. Wanting her, he finally fully recalled the long-ago passion of her responses, the ardor in her eyes, and the intensity of the memory shocked him.

The sight of her upturned face, filled with loathing, tore at his conscience until he knew he had to do something, anything, to stop the hate, if only for a second. Pinning her arms behind her, he held both her hands in one of his and drew her to his chest. The fingers of his free hand entangled themselves in her hair for more control and he bent to claim her lips with a mouth that insisted she respond. Mary's lips parted, her eyes wild and wide. His kiss grew harder, punishing her as well as himself.

Eric didn't know why he'd demanded what was no longer freely offered, any more than he could recall why he'd lost

control and made love to her in the first place. He only knew
he'd been a much bigger fool than he'd originally thought.
There was something about Mary—a hunger when he was
near her—that drove him to acts of passion he couldn't ra-
tionally explain and made him wonder what other delights
he might have been missing all these years.

Her sparse tears wet his cheek. The sorrow and remorse
he felt were crushing, the load of guilt a heavier burden than
he'd ever carried before. Somehow, someday, he swore he
was going to make it all up to her. He could do that by
helping Hope. If only Mary would let him.

Eric began to loosen his grip. *Oh, Mary,* his heart called
out, *please try to understand. I have to get to know my
daughter. She needs me.*

Mary wrenched away from him, her fingertips pressed to
her lips as if she'd just tasted bitter poison. Unable to stand
the sight of her disgust a moment longer, he swung aboard
the bay, kicked it hard in the flanks and rode down the hill.

Rubbing her reddened wrists, Mary fought to catch her
breath. The look on Eric's face as he'd turned to go had
been unfathomable. She closed her eyes to banish the vision and hugged herself, rocking back and forth, until all the
useless fire had left her soul and the sun, too, had set.

Leading her horse, she started slowly back to the barn. In
her deepest heart she knew Eric would keep his vow of silence. Beyond that, she would take life one day at a time,
just as she'd had to when her father and mother had
screamed at her for crushing all their grandiose hopes for
her career. She'd survive. Her parents' rejection had cut her
to the quick but it had also taught her to be self-sufficient.
There wasn't anything she set her mind to that she couldn't
accomplish. Alone. If Eric Lambert thought a few fierce
kisses were going to change that, he was in for a big surprise.

Chapter Five

The night was long and dream-riddled. Mary awoke before her alarm sounded, switched it off and sank back into her pillows, vaguely disturbed by a lingering feeling of disquiet. She didn't have to recall the details of her most recent dream to know Eric was a featured player; the imaginary rock in the pit of her stomach assured her he was.

The telephone beside her bed jangled and she hurriedly answered to keep the noise from waking Hope unnecessarily. It was John.

"Morning. Sleep well?" he asked.

"Fine, thanks. What's up? You never call me this early." She levered herself into a sitting position and folded her legs beneath the blankets.

"I'm going to run O'Malley at The Curragh this morning and I thought you and Hope would enjoy watching."

"Well . . ."

"Come on, Mary. Be honest. You're dying to go."

She couldn't help but laugh. "Know me pretty well, don't you?"

"That I do. And the girl, too. She'll be excited to see O'Malley on the track."

"You're right." Mary uttered a *humph* of resignation. "What time?"

"In an hour. Meet us at the stables and we'll all go together."

The hair on the back of Mary's neck prickled. "Us?"

"Lambert's riding, of course."

"Why doesn't that surprise me?"

"You don't like him very much, do you?"

"I don't really know him, Uncle John." Mary winced. Another white lie, added to her already overwhelming collection.

"All the more reason to go along, then. Maybe he'll grow on you."

"You mean, like fungus on a rock?"

John chuckled. "You're about that hard-headed sometimes, dear one. Must be a family trait. See you in an hour."

Mary lowered the receiver into its cradle. Being around Eric again had made her so darned cynical she was beginning to dislike herself, let alone him. That figured. Where he was concerned, she was playing the fool, as always. In spite of her past experiences, she was still attracted to him. Oh, she wasn't naive enough to call it love anymore, but the magnetism was there just the same.

She swung out of bed. She could simply refuse to go, ending her uncle's transparent attempts at peacemaking. Or she could keep her date at the stables and prove to herself that she was plenty strong enough to resist any temptation Eric presented.

"I am," she said forcefully. "It won't bother me a bit." Throw another lie on the pile, she thought, shaking her head in disgust. Go ahead. What's one more fib?

Mary stood quietly by the side of her bed and took a deep breath. To go would be folly, to *not* go, cowardice, and Mary Mulraney was no coward. She glanced at the clock on her nightstand. If they were going to be ready on time, she had better rouse Hope.

Padding barefoot down the hall, she peeked into the child's room.

Hope opened her eyes and blinked. "Hi."

"Hello, sleepyhead. You ready for breakfast? We have to hurry if we're going to go watch O'Malley run."

"We are? Where? When?"

"The Curragh. We leave in an hour."

"All right!" Jumping up, Hope rushed into the bathroom. "I'll hurry!"

"Wear your brown pants and yellow sweater," she called to the girl through the closed door. "And your good boots. You don't want to look like a tourist, and it can get pretty muddy in the paddock."

"Okay."

Quickly, Mary readied herself, too, by donning gray slacks and a soft pink sweater. Not that she'd stoop to putting on airs for the likes of Eric Lambert, she insisted. Neither did she want to embarrass John by not looking her best.

Mary set her jaw. More importantly, she was determined to use the opportunity the outing provided to convince Eric he had no inherent rights where Hope was concerned. The mere biological fact of parenthood didn't come with built-in privileges. Those, a man had to earn. In her opinion, Eric would never accumulate enough points in his favor to merit the closeness he'd said he intended to foster. He might as well learn to accept that fact as soon as possible. Today, for instance.

Mary stuffed a scarf into her soft leather purse and reached for her warm vest. It was blue nylon filled with down, serviceable and comfortable, but a tad tacky, she noted. Tossing it aside, she replaced it with the lilac-and-brown-toned tweed wool cape she wore mostly on Sundays. Its muted colors complemented her skin and hair, she knew, because wearing it never failed to attract compliments.

No use being purposely *less* attractive, either, she reasoned, telling herself she had a perfect right to dress however she liked. If her appearance bothered Eric, so much the better. It had apparently bothered him plenty already or he wouldn't have kissed her. Twice.

Mary shivered at the thought, the remembrance of Eric's warm, insistent mouth, his hard-muscled body pressed so tightly to hers. She'd been too incensed the night before to really notice the subtle changes in him, but now they played back in her memory in vivid detail. In retrospect, he'd seemed driven, more out of control than she'd ever seen him act before. And that look in his eyes. It was more than mere frustration and stubbornness. Mary couldn't put a name to it but neither could she forget it.

The slight softening of her opinion of him put her on her guard. She had to stay angry to keep her defenses up. Once she let herself begin to think kind thoughts about Eric she'd be lost. And so would Hope. The child had only one true protector, one guardian of her happiness—her. Mary might not be world famous, or rich, or as accomplished as Eric, but she was stronger-willed. She knew she was.

And it was her willpower, her solitary strength and determination, by which she would prevail. All she had to do was stand firm. Very soon, the time would come when he'd have to leave Ireland. Once he was gone, she and Hope could return to the peaceful life they'd enjoyed before he'd arrived to upset it.

And forget Eric? she asked herself.

The answer was a painfully easy no. Not a day had gone by since she'd lain in his arms in the straw that she'd not thought of him, yearned for what might have been. As time had passed, she'd replaced almost all of her tender feelings toward him with animosity. *Almost* all.

A familiar fluttering of her pulse caused her to press her lips together in a firm line. To be honest, traces of affection still lingered. There was something about him that both infuriated and excited her, a quality of danger more pronounced now than it had ever been when they were lovers.

She recalled the tender look in his eyes when he gazed at Hope. Therein lay the real danger. If Eric grew to love the child as his own, who knew what means he might use to become a more permanent part of her life. And then what? Competition? Traveling? Loneliness the likes of which only appeared now in Mary's worst nightmares? The thought shook her to the core. There was more at stake here than simply custody. Hope's whole life would be altered horribly if Eric began to influence it. Mary couldn't let that happen. She wouldn't.

"I'll ride in the car with Hope," Mary said.

John smiled and opened the passenger door of the older BMW for her. "You can keep me company, if you like, but I just saw Hope climb into the van with O'Malley."

"And with Eric?" Mary didn't have to ask to know.

"Most likely."

"Then I'll ride with them." She managed a smile. "Sorry, Uncle John. No offense."

He slammed the car door. "No problem. It'll be crowded, though."

"I'll manage."

Satisfied, John circled his car, got in and called out, "See you there," as he drove away.

Mary hurried to the van. Will sat behind the wheel, Hope was in the center and Eric was just getting in. They all stared at her.

"Uncle John ran off without me," she said, mentally crossing her fingers at the exaggeration and trying not to admire Eric in his tight, white riding breeches, high boots and black turtleneck. "So, I'll ride with you."

Eric stepped aside and raised one eyebrow. "Where?"

"Right here." She climbed in, tucking the folds of her long coat around her. "Scoot over, Hope."

The child wiggled accommodatingly but gave little ground. Glancing to her right, Mary could see that her presence left Eric less than six inches of seat cushion. She looked up and smiled apologetically. "Sorry."

He merely waited.

"I'll put Hope on my lap," Mary suggested, feeling terribly bright for having thought of it. Will grunted in the background.

"She needs to wear a seat belt," Eric said flatly.

Mary knew he was right. She'd always insisted Hope travel safely. "Then we'll scoot closer." She patted the narrow stretch of seat. "Come on. There's room."

"I have a better idea," Eric announced. "You get out."

"I will not!"

He took her arm. "Out. Come on. Don't take all day."

The satisfied grin he was flashing made Mary even more determined to hold her place. She strained against his pull. "You're not going to get away with leaving me here."

Eric chuckled. "That is a good idea. However, I have no intention of leaving you. One of us is going to ride on the other's lap. Either get out, or I'll get in and you'll be the one on the bottom."

"You wouldn't."

Hope had begun to giggle. "Do it, Eric!"

"Oh, yes, I would," he warned. "This seating arrangement was your idea, now move it."

Mary was out of the van in a flash. As she watched Eric climb in—in those damned tight pants—her throat tightened, her palms growing moist. My, the weather was warm for this early in the day. If she'd had a place to leave her good coat, she'd have shed it.

Settled, he held out his hand to her and she took it, letting him pull her up onto his lap. The door slammed. Eric's arms went around her.

"For safety," he said when she craned her neck to glare at him. "Let's go, Will, before Ms. Mulraney figures out a way to murder me in spite of the witnesses present."

William whistled. "Whew. Are you certain you're not Irish, boy? You know how to handle women."

Before Eric could answer, Mary made a sound of utter disgust. "You *handle* horses. Women are people, just like men, and should be treated with the same respect you give each other."

"Not *just* like men," Eric remarked. His hold on her tightened as he spoke, then loosened as Mary turned to look over her shoulder.

"Shut up, Lambert," she ordered. "There's a child present, you know."

He winked at Hope, who seemed to be enjoying the silly banter more than the adults. "Sorry, child. Living on a farm since you were born, I suppose you've never noticed there's a difference between mares and stallions. I hope I didn't upset you too much."

Hope giggled behind her hand and blushed.

Jabbing her elbow into Eric's ribs, Mary wiggled around to sit sideways so she could look at everyone more easily. Of course Hope knew the physical differences. Such things were obvious and had been explained matter-of-factly long ago to everyone's satisfaction.

"It wasn't outside differences I meant," Mary insisted.

Eric's grin was fading. "I know that." He moved his arms from around her and placed his hands at her waist. She continued to shift her weight. "Hold still."

"Why should I? You were the one who insisted I sit here."

His grip tightened, his voice husky. "Stop moving, Mary. Now."

She sobered, suddenly conscious of his predicament. The folds of her coat were not enough to mask Eric's reason for insisting so forcefully that she be still. A knot formed in her abdomen, twisting and coiling in an echo of his obvious desire, and she did as he asked.

The desire remained, her own as well as his, until they arrived at the racing grounds. Eric opened the door of the van and started to lift her off his lap.

Mary, too, was eager to break the embarrassing contact. She swung around and put her feet on the floor on the far side of his legs. As she slid to the ground, she glanced at his face. How she wished she hadn't!

Eric's eyes met hers, their emotion so poignant she could imagine an audible groan. Her hips were slipping away, their contact with his lap only momentary, yet he closed his eyes as if in pain. When he opened them again, Mary swore she glimpsed more than simple lust.

She looked away, not wanting to reveal her own reactions. In a moment she'd recover, she assured herself. After all, Eric Lambert wasn't the only man who'd ever demonstrated physical desire for her. Her heart missed a beat. Eric was the only one she'd ever succumbed to. That meant he had a hold over her, a ready-made inroad to her heart that no other man was privy to.

Mary turned away and started toward her uncle's parked car. All was not lost in spite of her unsettling memories of Eric. As long as he had no idea what his touch, his nearness was doing to her, he'd be perfectly safe. She paused in midstride. He would—but would she?

"This is where we run the Irish Sweeps Derby," John was saying. His arm swept in an arc. "It's basically a cross-country course. Our tracks are undulating, not flat like yours are in the States, and we run both left-and right-handed."

"And steeplechases?" Eric asked.

"All year long. You'll have to plan to come back in the winter and let me take you to Punchestown. It's in County Kildare, too."

"I'd like that." Eric glanced at Mary out of the corner of his eye. She knew, now, just how deeply her physical presence affected him. The question was, what would she do about it? An even better question was, what did *he* want to do about it? Damned if he knew.

Walking away beside John, Eric only half listened to the things the older man was telling him. Thoughts of Mary kept flooding his mind, distracting him, reminding him of their ride in the van. She'd been light, yet he'd felt as if he were bearing the weight of the world. And when she'd moved over him, bringing him to a hardness he hadn't wanted, hadn't planned, he'd been more embarrassed than she was.

Worse yet, his problem hadn't subsided as he'd expected it to when she'd held still. Nor was he totally rid of the reaction yet. At first, it had only happened when he was kissing her and he'd managed to hide it by stepping away. Now, it seemed the merest thought of Mary brought him to attention. The whole scenario was ridiculous. He was no randy teenager; he was a mature man. Surely he could control his urges.

Pulling himself back to the current moment, he listened as John said, "So I've arranged for you to take O'Malley over the course. It wasn't easy, mind you. Sandy Wilson's a tough trainer. But I explained how you needed an unfamiliar course to give the horse the fairest trial and he knuckled under as a favor to me."

Eric nodded. "He'll be running others at the same time?"

"Yes. Figured it'd be good for all the horses. He'll want to check you out, of course, even if you have won a fistful of medals."

"Understood." He glanced back over John's shoulder. Mary leaned on the fence, Hope beside her, watching horses pass as their riders warmed them up. Feeling himself responding to her once again, Eric quickly distracted himself. "Point me in the right direction and I'll go see Sandy. We might as well get started."

"I'll do you one better," John said, clapping him on the back. "While Will gets O'Malley ready, I'll introduce you around. After all, come next year you'll practically be my partner."

Eric hesitated, his brow furrowed. "I told you. I'm not sure a deal like that would work for us. We might be sorry."

"And if we don't make a stab at it?" John's laugh boomed. "I learned a long time ago that if a man waits around for good fortune to come up and camp on his doorstep, he's a fool. We make our own luck, son. Remember that. It's easy to sit back and let life just happen to you. It's chancy to take risks, but when you win, the victory is because of your own guts, not because of some shamrock in your pocket."

"You're right about winning," Eric said, keeping pace with him. "I agree. We make our own luck."

"I thought you'd see it that way." John grinned. "Yes, sir. I was just about positive of it."

Three horses came thundering past, their nostrils flaring, their manes flying, their shoes casting off great clumps of mud. Hope cheered. From her perch on the top rail of the fence she had a better view than Mary.

"Who's ahead?" Mary jumped up and down but couldn't get quite high enough to see the back side of the course.

"Eric!" Hope screeched. "He's murderin' them."

"O'Malley's good, all right," Mary remarked. "It's the horse that does the running, remember."

"Then how come Bounder beat Pint of Guinness?" Hope asked. "I heard you telling William."

"I must have been having a bad day and the horse sensed it. Besides, it takes more than one win to prove anything."

"Look!" In her excitement, the girl tried to stand and would have toppled off the fence if Mary hadn't steadied her. "Here they come. Eric's a mile ahead. Yeah! All right!"

Mary felt the ground beneath her feet trembling before she actually saw the horses. They crested a rise. Mr. O'Malley wasn't a mile ahead but he was a good, strong four or five lengths and responding beautifully. Eric had refused a whip, and Mary was overjoyed to see that it wouldn't have been needed, anyway. The horse had apparently taken to Eric the same way it had always obeyed Hope. It struck Mary funny that perhaps Mr. O'Malley had instinctively recognized the familial connection when no one else had a clue.

Passing the place where John and Sandy stood holding stopwatches, the horses slowed and all three riders waved.

Hope waved back. At the last minute, Mary, too, raised her hand. A good ride was a good ride. Eric deserved congratulations.

She was rewarded by the friendliest smile she'd received from him in a long time. It warmed her like the summer sun and her cheeks flushed in reply. No doubt about it, the man got to her, especially astride a good horse. Damn it.

John left his compatriot on the track and joined his family. "Not bad for a first run. They did the full two and a half miles."

"Bad?" Mary's voice rose. "Bad? It was amazing!"

"I thought so, too. It's nice to see that you agree." The older man chuckled.

She pulled a face. "You tricked me, you stinker."

"Not really. I just made it a little easier for you to say what you really thought without being so darned prejudiced and opinionated."

He had her there, Mary decided, blushing. Obviously she hadn't been doing such a wonderful job of hiding her feelings. "It was a good ride," she admitted. "There. Are you happy?"

"Ecstatic," her uncle said. Slipping one arm around Hope's waist, he let her put her arms around his neck and lifted her down off the fence. "Let's go, Leprechaun."

"Where?" The little girl took his hand and trotted to keep up.

"Yes, where?" Mary echoed. "O'Malley's run and won. What else is there?"

"Hurdles," John shot back over his shoulder. "We want to see how he does on a stadium course after putting so much into the race."

Mary had a premonition of disaster. There was more behind their morning outing than she'd guessed. Much more.

Jogging a few paces, she caught up with the others. "Why? What's the purpose?"

"To see if he's fit for Calgary, of course," John told her, grinning. "If I can get him into the Masters, I'll make an even bigger name for the farm."

"I don't suppose I need ask just who you had in mind to ride him." Mary's legs felt like she was carrying twenty-pound lead weights in her boots.

"I don't suppose you do." He patted her arm. "Cheer up. You don't have to go along. I can take good enough care of O'Malley by myself."

"You really think he has a chance?"

John smiled over at her. "You saw him run. What do you think?"

"That he has a lot better chance than we thought," Mary admitted. "But the Masters? Eric would need to train for months to ready a horse for that. And you don't have that long."

John nodded as he let go of Hope's hand. She hurried off to be closer to the upcoming action and he waited until she was too far away to overhear before he continued. "Even I had no idea O'Malley would do so well. I figured after Hope had been riding him so much, he'd be pretty much ruined for serious competition. I'm glad to see he's not."

That thought took Mary aback. She'd not considered Mr. O'Malley a contender before, and now she saw that as far as her uncle was concerned, the reverse was true. Yet he had been willing to sacrifice a promising horse for the sake of her little girl's happiness. The sensible businessman had made an emotional decision and was only now discovering he hadn't lost as much as he thought. Mary was not only happy for him, but his selfless act made her love him all the more.

She swung along in step with her dear uncle until they reached the railing where Hope waited. "Maybe Mr.

O'Malley won't be good enough or have enough energy left to make the jumps," Mary said. "In that case, Eric won't be able to use him."

"Eric will love my horse just like I do because Mr. O'Malley is wonderful. He'll jump. You'll see," Hope insisted.

Mary tousled the curly head and smiled. The way the big chestnut had responded to Eric on the track, she didn't doubt he'd jump. But there was more to eventing than simply clearing the gates, fences and hazards. It took skill and practice, and a horse that was in tune with his rider's every nuance, every wish. Such a relationship could take years to establish and hone. Anything less was miraculous.

By the time Eric had finished one round of hurdles, Mary knew that a miracle was exactly what she was seeing. She hadn't ridden professionally for years but she knew a championship combination when she saw one. Mr. O'Malley was bound for Canada. And Hope would miss him terribly. The only good part was that Eric would also be gone.

Looking out over the race grounds, Mary spied Eric aboard the chestnut gelding, and a lump formed in her throat. They'd had some good times in Calgary one spring; friendly times when he'd listened to her teenage problems and seemed more like a big brother than a lover. That was when she'd known, though, she reminded herself. That was when she'd decided that Eric Lambert was the one for her. The only one.

Whatever happened to the naive girl she'd been? Mary wondered. And where was the kind, gentle boy whose love she'd so coveted?

Her eyes drifted back to the track. Eric was much more mature now, more compelling, yet she yearned for a passing glimpse of the people they'd once been. In spite of her troubles with her parents and the resulting loneliness, those had been good times.

She closed her eyes to stop the visions. No, not good times. Tolerable times. Times made bearable because of the friendship of one boy. A boy who no longer existed.

Chapter Six

Mary thought better of forcing her presence in the van again, so she rode the short distance home with John. It was safe to relax her vigilance a bit. Eric would be leaving Ireland soon. He'd want to transport Mr. O'Malley to Alberta well before the competition to give the horse a chance to recover from the flight and get used to the climate and the differences in courses, especially the cross-country portions.

She leaned her head back against the tan leather seat of the BMW and closed her eyes. Watching Eric ride had opened a window into her soul, and sweet memories had fluttered out like brightly colored butterflies in a snowy field of daisies. No one who handled a horse the way he did could be all bad. He'd hurt her in the past, but part of that was her fault for assuming he returned her love simply because he'd whispered words of affection in the heat of passion. If she hadn't been so naive, so sheltered, she'd have seen the truth then, instead of assuming he was madly in love with her.

She sighed. Well, the least she could do was to wish him good luck now with Mr. O'Malley. That wasn't a weakening of her resolve, she insisted; it was plain courtesy and decent sportsmanship.

By the time John drove through the gates of home, she'd rehearsed and refined her speech at least twenty times. First, she'd compliment Eric on his skill. Then she'd tell him goodbye and wish him luck.

Her throat tightened, her nervousness and reluctance increasing as she pictured the scene, revising it once again. She'd congratulate him as planned. That much was safe. And she'd be so polite he'd probably drop over from the shock. But that was all the concession she dared make. And in the ensuing days until his departure, she'd stay the hell out of his way. Too many doses of Lambert charm and there was no telling what would happen to her already shaky emotional state. Mary wasn't about to hang around him like some horse-show groupie and find out.

Thanking her uncle for the ride, she had him drop her at the stables. Will was unloading Mr. O'Malley and Eric stood off to one side with Hope. Mary's heart did a flip and came to rest lodged in her throat. What a picture they made. Except for Eric's darker hair, they did look related; both were slim and carried themselves proudly.

And Hope had Lambert-green eyes. Mary shuddered. She'd often had a feeling that looking into her daughter's eyes was like looking into Eric's. Hope had always reminded her of him. From now on, the memories were going to be magnified beyond belief.

Mary skirted the van to stay out of Will's way as he led O'Malley to his stall. "Good ride," she told Eric. "I was impressed."

He smiled at her. "Coming from you, considering everything else, that's high praise."

"But well deserved," Mary said. She leaned down and whispered in Hope's ear. The little girl darted off to follow Will.

"What did you say to her?" Eric asked, slipping his hands into the pockets of a jacket he'd donned after riding.

"That somebody should tell Mr. O'Malley what a good job *he* did." Mary chuckled. "I figured she'd volunteer."

"There was a good chance of it."

Mary had begun to loosen up, and the compliments she'd intended to give were not hard to voice after all. In fact, she felt such admiration for Eric she expanded on them.

"I've never seen the horse perform better."

"Thank you."

"Your timing on the combination was flawless."

Eric's eyebrows arched. "You think so?"

"Yes. I wouldn't say it if I didn't mean it."

"You must." His voice deepened. "I don't believe you'd try to get to me with flattery. You're too honest for that."

The compliment shot straight to her guilty conscience and stuck there like a barb. She couldn't help the apologetic smile that lifted the corners of her mouth.

"And too stubborn."

Her smile grew. "That's true. I've changed a lot in the past seven or eight years, but my basic character traits are probably about the same."

"You're more beautiful," he said softly. "Yet there's a hard edge to you. Did I do that, Mary?"

Looking over her shoulder, she saw that Hope wasn't far away. "Let's walk a while. We can talk better if there are no little ears to overhear."

As they started to move off, Eric extended his arm, but Mary ignored it, choosing instead to walk apart from him. She plucked a blade of grass and ran it through her fingers. "I don't know that I can honestly blame you for anything specific," she said. "Even if a lot of the changes in my life were indirectly because of Hope, I did want a baby, someone who was mine to love."

"We were friends," Eric said. "You must know I never meant to hurt you. If you'd told me—"

"Told you?" She sighed and shook her head. "Told you what?" Pausing, she put out her hand and laid it lightly on his forearm. "What would you have done, Eric? Married me? Spirited me away?"

He shrugged. "I doubt it. In those days I was pretty immature and a darned sight more self-centered. All I thought about was my career and the next win. Nothing else mattered."

"I know. I found that out the hard way." Mary released her hold on him and started walking again. "And where would that have left me? I'd already been rejected by you once. Even in my confused state, I knew I couldn't take another blow like that. You meant too much to me."

"But why Ireland? Surely you could have stayed in the States."

"It doesn't matter now. Hope and I are happy. We have each other and the horses we both love. It's a good life, Eric. It is."

"I know that and I'm relieved you see it clearly, too. You have the best here—both horses and people—and your aunt and uncle are super."

"That they are." She scuffed her boot in the mud and stared down the narrow lane.

"But what about you, Mary? What about later?"

Her gaze raised to meet his. "Later?"

"When you're forty, or fifty, or more. When Hope has grown up and made a life of her own. What then?"

"That's a long way off. I don't borrow trouble," she told him. "I deal with problems as they arise and not before."

"You don't plan?" Eric shook his head. "I do. By the time I was sixteen, I thought I knew exactly where my life was going and how it would end up."

"I remember that you had big dreams," she said. "I didn't realize you were living by them, though."

"Not by them, *for* them. They ruled me, Mary. My career dominated my entire life."

"You're talking as if it doesn't anymore." She smiled knowingly at him. "If that's the case, why did you come all the way to Ireland to talk to John about his horses?"

"Fate maybe? Hell, I don't know. But I'm glad I did."

"I'm not," she said honestly. "It would have been so much better if we'd never met again."

"If I'd never met Hope?"

"Yes." She thrust out her chin.

Studying her, assessing her mood first, Eric reached out and took her hand. "Your fingers are ice-cold." He rubbed them between his palms.

"Eric, I . . ."

"We can't go back, Mary," he said. "Even if we wanted to, we couldn't."

"I don't want to."

He could see that she meant every word. "I don't either. We were two stupid kids and the only thing we didn't mess up was Hope. She's wonderful."

"Your career wasn't ruined," Mary said, rescuing her hand and stepping back, away from the potent tug of his masculinity. "Mine was."

"Only because you dropped out and ran away to try to hide your pregnancy."

"Even if there hadn't been that element of secrecy, I wouldn't have endangered my baby's welfare by continuing to jump hurdles. I couldn't. You should know that."

"There were other steps you could have taken," he said very quietly. By the shocked, distressed look on Mary's face, Eric knew he'd overstepped the bounds of their tenuous truce, but it was too late to reclaim the careless thought and keep it from being uttered.

"Oh, God, no! Look at her, Eric. Think about her. You said yourself that she's a wonder. Are you telling me I should have seen to it that she was never born?" Mary's eyes widened in horror. "The thought of my world with no Hope in it is like picturing heaven without angels."

"I know. I'm sorry." And he was. Mary had jolted him to his marrow when she'd suggested a world without the darling daredevil he'd so recently sworn to protect and nurture. He didn't want to take her from Mary, yet he also had begun to visualize the child as part of his own life. An integral part. Hope was more than the sum of her two parents. Much more. So what was he going to do about it? They'd agreed they couldn't go back. Maybe they could go forward.

"Have you ever thought of getting back into competition?" he asked, feigning nonchalance.

Mary's mouth dropped open. "You're kidding. At my age? No way."

"Your age? You can't be much over twenty-five."

"That's close. Anyway, the answer is still no."

"Why not?" He warmed to his subject. "You could take Hope to some events and do a little riding of your own, on the side."

"Take *Hope* to events? Over my dead body!"

He held up his hands. "Okay, okay. Then you could both come to watch me ride."

"And have everyone find out about her? Taunt her with it? Or are you figuring that once she's experienced the thrill of eventing I won't be able to keep her happy at home?"

Mary couldn't believe he was unaware of the possible ram-
ifications of what he was suggesting.

"You're not being reasonable," Eric argued. "Hope's
secret is safe with me and I'm sure you're not going to blab,
so what's the problem? Surely you don't intend to keep her
isolated on this farm forever." Just when he thought he was
beginning to understand Mary, to make progress with her,
something like this came up. It was plain from her stance
and the determination in her face that she was adamantly
against anything he proposed. If he'd said it was raining,
she'd have sworn the sky was clear.

"I'll keep her as isolated as I have to," she countered.
"Accept it, Eric. Hope isn't going to follow in my footsteps
or yours, and that's final."

"Fine. Keep her prisoner."

"Prisoner? Just who do you think you are, accusing me
of such a terrible thing?"

"I'm her father."

"That's the whole problem, isn't it?"

"Problem? It's no problem for me, Mary. I've accepted
my place in the background. I just won't sit quietly and
watch you ruin her life, that's all."

Mary paced away from him, then whirled, her fists
clenched. "She's happy, damn it. Why can't you believe
that?"

Lowering his voice, Eric stared at her. "Because it isn't so.
Or at least it won't be as she gets older. Think about it.
Here's a child with the potential for greatness and the financial backing to reach the top in her field, yet for personal reasons, her mother keeps her from it. How's she
going to feel about that when she's old enough to figure it
out for herself? The few lessons you may eventually give her
won't be enough and you know it."

Mary pressed her palms over her ears. "Stop it."

"No." Grasping her wrists, he pulled her hands away. "You're going to listen to me. I think Hope takes the chances she does to prove to you she's a great rider."

"That's nonsense."

"Is it? I don't think so. And I could never forgive myself if she was hurt and I'd done nothing to prevent it."

"Forgive yourself?" Mary's voice rose and quavered. "Forgive yourself? Like when you led me on and slept with me, then promptly forgot all about it?"

He loosed his grip and stepped back so she wouldn't bolt. "I was young. Stupid. I thought you'd be as sorry it happened as I was, so I tried to put it all behind me as soon as possible. If Hope hadn't been conceived, you'd probably have done the same thing."

As he gazed at Mary's expression, he quickly realized how wrong he was. And then he remembered her words when she was describing Hope's father. She'd said she loved him. Him. Not some faceless, fictitious character, but him. She'd opened her heart and, once again, he hadn't absorbed the real truth in her words until too late.

Mary was watching his face closely. She saw the new realization come over him and was surprised that he was just now becoming aware of how deeply she'd been hurt.

He reached out his hand to her but she ignored the gesture. "Oh, honey. I never dreamed..."

"No. You didn't." His penitence wasn't enough to make her change her mind about how to best raise Hope. It did, however, help soften her anger toward him. "You really didn't, did you? And I loved you so much."

Eric was shaking his head. He ran his fingers through his hair. "Guess I was an even bigger fool than I'd thought."

"No. You were honest about your feelings. Looking back, I can see it was for the best."

He sighed, then thrust his hands into his pockets. "No matter what you think of me, I do care about Hope. And I'm right. If you try to shelter her from the whole world, she'll come to view you as her jailer, the same way you used to tell me you felt about your parents."

That, Mary couldn't accept. "They made me travel to shows so I could perform to feed their egos. That's entirely different."

"The actions may be different, but the motivations are the same. Instead of looking at what *you* wanted, they imposed their wills. For guidance, it's a parent's duty to do that. The rub comes when the parent forgets that the child has a mind and desires of its own."

"Hope is far too young to be making decisions like that."

"But she's not too young to be introduced to the opportunities that are available so that she can one day make an educated choice."

"Forget it." Mary squared her shoulders. "It's a long way to Canada, Mr. Lambert. After you return, and on future visits, you can continue to visit Hope as I promised, but that's all." Her tone grew more serious as she recalled his prior warnings. "I'll make sure I give you no excuse to betray me."

"Oh, for..." Muttering epithets, Eric wheeled around and left her. He had to, before he said something he'd regret. Betray her? How could she think such a thing? The progress he thought he'd made with Mary counted for nothing if she still distrusted him. Yet, if he showed any weakness or confessed how much his affection for her and the child had blossomed since his arrival, he'd be taking an awful chance. Until she demonstrated some reciprocation of feelings, he didn't dare bare his own or she'd know how much influence she actually had with him; how much her happiness mattered.

It was ironic how their situations had reversed. Now he was the one who cared and she was the one to whom their relationship mattered little. He didn't like the off-balance feeling that realization gave him. He ran his fingers through his hair. Mary had the emotional and physical advantage over him because she'd be keeping Hope at home in Ireland while he and John went to Calgary. Or would she?

Quickening his steps, he headed for the main house. Mr. O'Malley was a special favorite of Hope's. Maybe John could be persuaded to invite the child to go along. And just maybe, if that didn't make Mary so mad she strangled him outright, Eric mused, she'd also agree to make the trip. He had to do something to try to jolt her from her safe little cocoon, for her sake, if not for his own. She deserved more breadth and color in her life and so did Hope. Eric had a whole exciting world to show his daughter.

He noticed he was breathing harder than the brisk walk would have normally warranted. It was because of the vision, he deduced, the picture in which there were three happy people. Hope, himself . . . and Mary Mulraney.

There were moments when he scoffed at the idea, but they were becoming fewer and fewer as he got to know the woman she'd become. Was there a chance for them? he wondered. And was that what he truly wanted? A large lump of tension behind his solar plexus was the only answer his body or mind provided.

Eric snorted a derisive chuckle and shook his head. Some planned life, he groused. How the hell was he going to convince Mary of what was right for them when he didn't have a clue himself?

A sense of finality had settled over Mary after Eric had walked her home. For the first time since he'd popped back into her life like a scene from a familiar movie, she'd begun to really believe everything was going to turn out all right. She'd told him where she stood and he'd finally stopped issuing stubborn rebuttals. Consequently, when her aunt knocked on her door, she felt no apprehension whatsoever.

"I would have telephoned," Katie said, stepping inside and sliding the scarf from her head to shake it out, "but Eric said you'd gone home, and when I saw the chance to sneak away without John catching on, I just took it."

"Sneak away?" Mary giggled. "You sound like a spy."

Katie made her way into the living room and pointed toward the kitchen. "How about a cup of tea?"

"Sure. Sounds like old times. We did get to know each other pretty well over hot tea and cookies, didn't we?" She squeezed the older woman's hand. "In case I haven't told you lately, thanks."

"You haven't, but that's no matter. We were glad to help. Anyhow, I didn't come here to discuss the past." Seating herself, Katie rested her elbows on the simple pine table and cupped her chin in her hands. "I'm beginning to wonder if my poor John is getting senile."

"Uncle John? No way. He's as sharp as when I first met him," Mary said, putting the kettle on to boil.

"In that case, it's even worse." She didn't smile. "This Lambert business really has me scalded."

Mary understood the local idiom for 'vexed.' "Me too."

"And you have no notion what it's all about?" Katie made a funny face. "Oh, dear. I'd hoped you'd have some idea after your ride the other evening."

Telling herself she was doing the right thing by continuing to withhold the sordid truth about her past from her aunt, Mary proceeded to gather her tea things. The arguments she'd had with Eric had nothing to do with her uncle's original reason for inviting him, and John's motives were what Katie was curious about.

"I'm sure it's as Uncle John said—he just wants to improve his breeding stock and make a bigger name for the farm by trading on Eric's reputation."

With a quick shake of her head, Katie dismissed the breeding-stock idea. "The famous part, maybe. Not the other. We've never discussed our finances with you, Mary, but if the truth be known, John could buy almost any horse he wanted and have plenty of money left over."

"I see." She smiled as she poured hot water into two bone-china cups and set them on the table. "Well, at least I feel better about all the years I've lived here."

"You've worked hard for your keep." Katie absently dunked a tea bag in and out of her cup.

"No amount of work can buy what you and Uncle John gave me," Mary said quietly. "I never felt a part of any family till I moved here and met you."

"Have you heard from your parents?" Katie asked, laying one hand over Mary's. "I thought maybe, on Hope's last birthday..."

"No."

"You did write, didn't you? You told me you were planning to."

Mary got up to fetch her cookie jar, more for something to do than a desire for sweets. "I wrote. I didn't mail the letter, though."

"Why ever not?"

Taking a peanut-butter cookie, she pushed the jar toward Katie. "What's the point? They made it clear I'd ruined all their plans for me, or rather, Hope had. She's very dear to me, Aunt Katie. If they don't accept her, I can't accept them, either."

"I do understand." She fished around in the jar. "Oops. Two stuck together. Guess I'll have to eat them both."

Mary smiled. "I guess you will."

Chewing, Katie looked thoughtful. "But I've gotten off the track, haven't I? I still don't see how Eric fits into my husband's plans."

"Who can say?" Mary remained outwardly calm without too much difficulty. Of all the people in her life, Katie was the easiest to talk to. It wouldn't hurt to disclose a tiny bit of carefully censored truth. "At shows, everybody hung around the same haunts. I'd seen Eric a few times in the old days and John probably met him that way, too. My parents always discouraged my friendships, though. They said they distracted me from my work." She managed a chuckle. "The only time they seemed interested in me was when I was winning. Then, there they were, taking bows and pointing proudly to *their* daughter."

"And that's why you don't want Hope to compete?"

"Partly," Mary said, taking a bite of cookie and a swallow of tea. "She needs the stability of a home, like this one. All children do. That's missing on the circuit."

"For you it was," Katie said wisely. "But Eric seems to have weathered it okay."

"Some do, I suppose. It's not a chance I'm willing to take with my daughter, that's all."

"Makes sense to me." With an understanding nod, the older woman took a moment to quietly sip her tea. "Please remember that John's actions are based on his love for you and Hope. That's why he wants her to learn from the best."

"I know that. I'm sorry I made such a scene at dinner the other night."

"That's one of the reasons I thought it would be wise to pay you a little private visit." She scrunched up her face. "As a good Irish wife, I shouldn't be here telling you this."

Sudden apprehension filled Mary. So, there was another reason for Katie's unexpected appearance. "Telling me what?"

"Now, don't get upset. I disapprove, but there's nothing I can do. John is my husband."

"What?" The volume of Mary's voice rose.

Katie grimaced and reached for Mary's hand. "Your Uncle John plans to ask Hope to go to Calgary with him and Mr. O'Malley."

Mary paced the floor for nearly an hour after Katie left. She was beginning to feel like a Ping-Pong ball in a tournament match. Just about the time she thought she had matters well in hand, *whack,* back she went the other way. Well, she was through being batted around by chance, or people, or whatever forces were at work in her life. It was time to take charge.

Whether or not Eric was implicated in John's decision to ask Hope to travel to Calgary, as she suspected he was, she did concede he might be right about her tendency to overprotect the child. As she saw it, she had two choices. Either she could wait for John to issue his invitation and let herself be put in the position of having to raise the roof, or she could take the initiative and make the same suggestion first, and see what happened.

She shivered, remembering the time she'd spent in Calgary with Eric so long ago. He may have forgotten all about it, but she hadn't. Oh, no. She remembered the summer before the fateful Olympics in Los Angeles with heartrending intensity. But she still wanted to make the trip. Hope must be made to see, once and for all, that her mother was no insensitive jailer. The whole idea was abhorrent.

Pausing, Mary listened to the truths stirring deep within her soul. Maybe she had been too strict in some ways, too lenient in others. That was the trouble with motherhood—there were no trial runs. You had to practice on the baby. Hopefully, before the child grew up, you had figured out how becoming the perfect parent was supposed to be accomplished.

She nodded and took a deep, confident breath, her decision solid. Tackling the upcoming trip head-on wasn't only for Hope's benefit. Mary had something to prove, too. She owed herself the chance to demonstrate that the past could no longer harm her.

The place to do that was Calgary.

With Hope.

And with Eric.

Chapter Seven

The enormous amount of energy she'd expended pacing, thinking, planning and raving semicoherently, alone in her living room, served to calm Mary appreciably by dinnertime. Truth be told, by evening she was totally at peace. Taking stock of the others gathered around the table, she decided she was the most in control, except possibly for Hope, who seemed as happy-go-lucky as ever.

John cleared his throat. "Mary. I have a proposition for you."

She smiled sweetly. "Really? Well, before we get into that, I was wondering if I might ask a favor?"

"Of course."

Blotting her lips on her napkin, she looked straight at Eric for a moment, then transferred her attention to Hope. "First, though, I need to know if my daughter would like to take a trip." Out of the corner of her eye she noted the quizzical look on Eric's face.

"To the zoo?" Hope asked. "You said we'd go there sometime."

"No, honey. To Calgary with Mr. O'Malley... that is, if it's okay with your Uncle John."

"Oh, wow!" Hope clapped her hands. "Sure!"

"Well, John?" Mary pivoted her gaze to him. "Is there room?"

"We'll make room!" he boomed. "What a wonderful idea."

It was hard for Mary to keep from chuckling as she saw the astonished look on Eric's face. That, coupled with John's suspicious glance at Katie and Katie's totally convincing aura of innocence, made the entire picture terribly funny. Too bad she didn't dare laugh.

"Then it's settled? Good." Mary returned to her dinner.

Eric was the first to find his voice after the initial shock wore off. Guilt overrode his usually good sense. "If Hope needs anything for traveling, I'll be glad to chip in."

Mary gritted her teeth but remained outwardly calm and collected. "I can buy anything extra my daughter may need or want. I do work here, you know."

"It was a friendly offer. I never meant to imply you didn't take care of her." Eric looked to his mentor for direction but got only a confused shake of John's gray head.

Continuing to eat slowly, Mary was aware all eyes were on her. "I think I'll take Hope into Dublin tomorrow," she said, as if to herself. "We can do a little shopping. Katie can come along if she wants. It might be fun for us to get away. We haven't done anything like that in a long time."

Still, Mary's voice held no hint of sentiment other than calm determination. That was more than enough. She looked up to address her uncle straightforwardly. "You can see to Hope's airline ticket for me when you book the horse's transportation, but I want it understood that I'll pay you back.''

"If that's what you want.'' He held up his hand to silence Eric when he saw him start to open his mouth.

Mary nodded. She hadn't missed the silent exchange between the two men, and seeing it served to strengthen her resolve and sharpen her wits even further. A conspiracy was no longer mere supposition on her part. Eric had tried to manipulate her, through John, just as she'd surmised. It was clearly time to finish shocking them both as they deserved.

"It is,'' she said flatly. "As for my seat, it had better be next to Hope's.''

Eric couldn't keep silent any longer. *"Your* seat?''

"Yes. My seat.'' She took a long draft of wine, dabbed her lips, then replaced the napkin in her lap. "You didn't think for a minute I'd let Hope go without me, did you?''

"I don't know what I thought,'' he said, his tone level. "You seemed so determined never to leave Ireland, I just supposed . . .''

"I'm sure you did.'' The full force of her maternal ire returned. In complete control, Mary fixed her gaze on Eric without flinching. She wasn't going to run away, nor was she going to sit there like a lamb and let them all think she was too dense to see what they'd tried to do. The men had set the rules but she wasn't about to be done in by them. Not by a long shot.

She fairly bristled. "You thought I was going to send my little girl all that way alone? Really, Mr. Lambert. You should know me better than that by now. I've told you how I feel about my daughter often enough in the past few days. Where Hope goes, I go. Is that clear?''

"Perfectly.'' He raised his wineglass in a toast. "To Calgary and winning.''

"To *winning*," Mary repeated, reaching across to touch the lip of her goblet to his. "Something we both understand all too well."

Mary had gravitated to the kitchen after dinner to help clean up. The warm room and Katie's company offered camaraderie and solitude, two things she knew she needed. Drying a plate, she slipped it onto the stack in the cupboard.

Up to her elbows in suds, Katie smiled over at her niece. "You really surprised me tonight, girl, and I already had a clue." She giggled. "Did you see the looks on the men's faces?"

Mary grinned. "How could I miss them? Uncle John almost fell off his chair! It was all I could do to keep from busting up laughing."

Katie sobered. "You've made a big decision. Are you sure about Calgary?"

"I'm sure."

"Then we'll go into Dublin, like you said. Sounds like a good excuse to have high tea at the Shelbourne."

Mary chuckled. "Uncle John will have a fit. That place is *so* expensive."

"I know. It'll serve him right." Shaking her head, she finished washing and rinsing the last piece of silverware and let the water out of the sink. "I still think the man is getting daft."

"He's a man," Mary remarked wryly. "They never make sense to me."

"Nor us to them, more's the pity. Although, there are times I'm glad your uncle doesn't know what's going on in my head."

"That is a good point." Folding the damp towel and draping it over a rod beside the counter, Mary slipped into her down vest. "And speaking of men, I imagine Will is fit to fire me. I didn't show up at the barn to help exercise the horses this afternoon and I feel really bad about it. If we're all done here, I'll go on down and try to catch up on some of my work before it gets dark."

"Of course, dear. You needn't have bothered with this. We each have chores to do, and the dishes are mine. It gives me a sense of worth around here, especially since I don't ride."

Mary kissed her cheek and took her leave. "I know. Tonight I needed the extra time to unwind, though."

"I hope it helped."

"You always help, Katie. You always did."

"Take care," she called as Mary walked to the door and let herself out into the misty evening.

There was a chill in the air, a quiet afoot that seemed the harbinger of a storm. Just like when Eric had walked her home, Mary mused. She'd dropped her guard and he'd nearly convinced her that all he wanted was to see Hope once in a while when he visited Ireland. She should have known better. No one as competitive as Eric would ever be satisfied with second place.

The barn area wasn't totally deserted. Neither was it the hub of activity she'd expected. Across the stable yard, John and Eric strolled in front of the line of stalls, Hope following closely behind.

Mary scowled. Continuing to get the best of Eric was going to be more complicated since John had begun to interfere. For an instant that afternoon, she'd considered telling her family why she wanted no more to do with Eric Lambert, but she'd quickly dismissed the idea as a bad one. Both her aunt and uncle had strict moral standards. If they found out Hope was illegitimate, it might adversely color their feelings toward the girl, just as it had Mary's parents'. She couldn't take the chance.

Reading the latest entries on the checklist posted in the tack room, Mary realized Will had assigned others to do her work that day. In a way, she was grateful because of her growing fatigue. In another way, she was sorry she had no specific tasks to occupy her time or her mind.

"Get used to it," she muttered to herself, stuffing her hands into the pockets of her vest and starting for home. Except for the short distraction of going to Dublin for the day, she was going to have far too much time to worry, to imagine what Eric's next move might be. It was worse than knowing for sure that something bad was going to happen—it was like sensing danger and not being able to see it well enough to know which way to dodge to avoid it.

The sound of a horse's hooves on the path behind her took her by surprise due to the lateness of the hour. She gave ground, expecting the rider to pass by. He didn't. When she realized who it was, she understood.

"I saw you from the stables," Eric said. "So I made the excuse of wanting to try Pint of Guinness and came after you."

"Why?"

"Good question." Dismounting, he took the horse's reins and led him along behind as they walked. "I guess I wanted to be sure you were still speaking to me."

"Why shouldn't I be?"

"Because I had already suggested to John that he take Hope to Canada. When you turned the tables on us, I imagined you'd found out."

"Maybe. Maybe not."

"Are you angry?"

Pausing, she stared at him in the light of the setting sun. His skin glowed, his eyes twinkled, and there was a little-boy quality to the expression on his face. At that special moment, she didn't think she could have stayed unwaveringly mad at him if he'd been Jack the Ripper, about to do her in. There was a gentle, tender quality about Eric that spoke directly to her heart without bothering to involve her rational mind. Thinking quickly, she manufactured a plausible excuse for her recent demonstrations of civility.

"I can't afford to stay openly angry with you. How would I explain it? You yourself warned me about Hope's inquisitive mind and you were right. Sooner or later, she'd start to ask too many direct questions."

"So, you're going to become her shadow?"

"If that's what it takes."

He reached into his pocket. "Then at least let me help you with the expenses. I stopped at the airport and changed some money. Here."

"Put it away," she ordered.

"Don't be silly. You can't have much saved with what your uncle pays you."

Bristling, Mary put her hands on her hips and faced him. "My uncle rescued me from disaster, gave me a home, a job and love I'd never had before. He's often tried to raise my wages and I've refused, so don't you go putting him down, you hear?"

"I didn't mean it that way." Eric still clutched a handful of pound notes. "Just take these and get Hope some new clothes."

"Which reminds me," Mary said, finally raising her voice. "What was the idea of offering me money at dinner with everybody sitting there, taking it in? You sounded like a guilty father, for heaven's sake."

The grin which spread across Eric's face was accompanied by a deep-seated feeling of warmth. "You think so? I didn't mean to, of course, but I have been thinking along

those lines. We'll need to set up a fund of some sort for
Hope so I can begin to help support her.''

"No. No way. She doesn't need you or your money.''

"If not now, what about college? Surely you won't deny
her a source of tuition.''

"That's a long way off.''

"Then put the money in the bank and save it for her.'' He
was beginning to lose his cool. "What is the matter with
you? Be sensible for a change.''

"Oh, I am, Mr. Lambert. Believe me, I am. Once I let
you give me support for Hope, your position as her supposed father will be strengthened and I don't intend to let
that happen. I've never actually told you she's yours, you
know. Maybe she isn't.''

Eric shook his head. "It won't work, Mary. All you have
to do is look at us together to see the truth, and you know
it.'' He snorted. "Hell, most of the time she acts more like
me than she does you.''

"She does not.''

"Does, too.''

The ridiculous scenario they were playing out reminded
Mary of kids squabbling in a playground, not two mature
adults discussing their offspring. Suddenly, the whole matter, coming so close on the heels of her suppressed mirth
during dinner, struck her as too funny to ignore. A giggle
was forming in the back of her throat, dispelling the animosity she'd tried so hard to nurture. Lord, they sounded
just like silly, stubborn children!

To illustrate her point she put her hands on her hips, made
a face and stamped her foot. *"Does not."* The waiting giggles erupted and the puzzled look that resulted on Eric's face
made the whole situation even funnier.

"I take it you're telling me I'm behaving badly.''

Mary continued to laugh, the action a much-needed release for her built-up tension. "You always were a spoiled-
rotten kid."

"I was not."

"See?"

"Well, maybe." He sighed. Happier times with her were
flooding back into his memory and he wished they could
share the same kind of rapport now. "What are we going to
do, Mary?"

"I don't know about you," she countered, smiling and
catching her breath, "but I'm going to go see what I need to
buy before we all fly to Canada." Pulling a face, she started
for home once again.

Eric thought it best to let her change the subject, do things
her way for the present. "You'll have a good time. You'll
see." He fell into step beside her, watching the different expressions that flitted across her lovely face.

"Probably," she finally admitted. "It's been a long time
since I've been much of anywhere."

"I'll take care to protect Hope from anyone who's overly
curious," Eric promised. "I don't want her hurt, either, in
spite of what you think."

Slowly, Mary turned to face him. "What I think? Do you
really want to know what I think?"

"Yes." He hoped she was aware of how deeply he meant
it.

"I think you're beginning to love Hope, just like I do."
The truth of her conclusion was affirmed in his eyes. When
he nodded, she went on. "And I think you're trying to figure out a way to become a more important, permanent part
of her life because you've only recently realized what you've
been missing all these years."

"Biological clock?"

"Something like that." Firmly yet tenderly, Mary laid her hand on his forearm. "Know this, Eric. I am Hope's mother and I have raised her alone for over seven years. I don't want to share her, but more importantly, I don't want to lose her. Legally, she's mine."

"I realize that."

"Then remember this, too. I was a tough competitor in the arena when all I had at stake was a trophy or a blue ribbon. Winning this current contest between us is much more important. I don't intend to lose."

"Or compromise?"

The question wasn't unexpected. She'd already thought out her stand. "Not any more than I have to in order to preserve Hope's happiness, no. As long as you hold to your promise of silence, I'll continue to keep my end of the bargain and let you visit her."

"But no more?" Eric already knew the answer. Yet his heart insisted he ask.

"No. No more."

He put his hand over hers. "What about your feelings, Mary? The more I'm around you, the more I realize what we might have had once, if I hadn't been so blind. Don't tell me the same idea hasn't occurred to you."

Shaking her head, she pulled away. "You still don't get it, do you? No, I didn't think you would."

By backing up, she put distance between them while staring into his eyes. The poignancy of their situation had called up volatile emotions on both sides and she had to have more room to breathe or she'd suffocate under the weight of its intensity.

She stood fast as his eyes called to her, beckoned her into his embrace, into his life. If she'd been the only one affected, she might have gone to him. But her desires were not the important issue. Eric wanted Hope, and Mary saw that if she conceded anything, his way would be open. She couldn't let that happen.

"You're right," he said slowly. "I don't get it. I can see you still feel something for me. Why are you so afraid to find out how deep it goes or what may come of it if you let yourself go?"

"Have you ever quit in the middle of a cross-country event?" she asked. "Just pulled up short and stopped competing?"

"No. But what has that got to do with us and with Hope?"

"Everything. I started on this course before she was born and made my choices according to what I thought was best for her. Nothing has changed."

Soberly, Eric stopped following Mary and let her edge farther away. "You've never run this kind of race before," he said, picking up the analogy. "Suppose you've miscalculated and you're wrong?"

"It'll still be my best," she countered. Turning her back, she started up the flower-edged walk to her cottage. Just as she closed the front door behind her, she heard Eric say, "And mine."

By the time Hope wandered home that evening, Mary had most of the child's clothes spread out on the bed and piled on the rug. It was evident that even if they hadn't had the trip to Calgary coming up, she'd have needed to go shopping soon, simply because Hope had grown so much taller lately.

"Try these on," Mary told her, pointing. "And these. I'll get paper and a pencil and make a list so we'll know exactly what to look for when we go to town."

"Okay." Hope slipped out of her boots and shed the pants she'd worn all day. When Mary started to pick them

up, the girl ran to stop her. "Don't wash those. Not yet."
Hope fished in the pockets and pulled out a wad of bills.

"What's that?" Mary had a strong suspicion where the
money had come from and the thought rankled.

"Eric gave it to me," Hope said. "For shopping."

"You'll have to give it back."

"Why?"

Lifting the child's chin, Mary looked into her eyes. Eric's eyes. "Because we don't take gifts from strangers."

"Eric's not a stranger. He's my friend."

"We still don't know him well enough to accept gifts,"
she explained. "It was very wrong of him to offer, especially after I told him not to."

Hope began to grin. "I could save the money for our trip.
Eric says we'll all have a wonderful time. And he's going to
take me to a place where they have rides, and a real old-
fashioned train, and animals, and—"

"Heritage Park," Mary murmured.

"Uh-huh. That's the name."

"Go get the clothes I told you to try on," Mary said, her
emotions held in tenuous check.

"What about the money?"

"I'll return it for you tomorrow. Now get dressed."

Heritage Park, Mary mused. Calgary. It was a balmy
summer day when Eric had talked her into going there with
him and a group of other young riders instead of practicing
dressage as her parents had instructed. She'd stolen away
and spent the entire afternoon following Eric around; a
blissfully sweet, innocent afternoon never to be repeated,
she noted sadly.

The parental fury she'd encountered upon her return had
been enough to keep her from engaging in such lovely folly
for a long time after that. Yet her infatuation with Eric had

continued to grow, fueled by her fantasies, until the next summer when they'd met again in Los Angeles.

The vision was as clear as a photograph. The equestrian events of that particular Olympics had been split between Santa Anita Park in Arcadia and Fairbanks Country Club, near San Diego, stretching the officially three-day event into one actually taking six days to stage. And while her parents and their crew had been busy helping transport horses between sites, she'd managed to sneak over to see Eric again. Managed to make him love her.

Tears filled her eyes. If only he really had loved her, how differently everything might have turned out.

"Mama?" Hope stood, dressed as she'd been instructed, studying her mother's tears.

Mary quickly wiped her damp cheeks.

"What's wrong, Mama?"

"Nothing. I'm fine."

Wrapping her thin arms around Mary's waist, the little girl clung to her and patted her back. "Don't cry, Mama. I still love you the most. Honest, I do. I'm sorry I took the money. I won't ever do it again."

"It's okay, honey. I love you, too." Mary hugged her tightly. For how long will you love me, unquestioningly, like this? she wondered. I know it's best for both of us to put Eric out of our lives and yet I can't stop dredging up loving thoughts of him in spite of myself. If I can't control my feelings, knowing what I know, how can I expect you not to love him, too?

Chapter Eight

Eric had felt out of sorts since Mary had thrust the crumpled wad of bills he'd given Hope into his hand and stormed off without a word. He'd seen her leave a little later, bound for Dublin with Hope and Katie.

Working with Mr. O'Malley had helped distract him, yet still there was the nagging sense that some vital part of him was gone. It didn't take a genius to figure out he missed Mary—and Hope. When he had let himself become involved in their lives, he hadn't realized how much they, in turn, would affect his.

At the outset, he'd expected to simply conclude his current business in Ireland, board a plane and fly back home to get on with his life the way it had been. He'd planned to keep in touch, of course, send money for Hope, and continue to tend to his career, his plans for the future.

That wasn't going to be quite what happened, now, he saw with a modicum of chagrin. Mary had only been gone for a few hours and already he missed her so much he could taste it. Was that love? he wondered. Would love have made him lonely in the midst of all the activity on Day's farm? Was that why he thought of Mary, wanted to touch her, to hear her voice, almost every waking moment?

Eric cursed. Where had he gotten such stupid ideas? Love was fun. It was pleasurable. It was supposed to make a man feel ten feet tall, lift his spirits until they soared, heal the scars of the past. Wasn't it? Well, wasn't it?

Damned if he knew. He'd had his share of women, before and after Mary, but none of the others had ever made his palms sweat or left him tongue-tied or caused such a painful knotting in his gut. If he hadn't experienced it, he wouldn't have believed it. When Mary had driven away in the old BMW, he'd been seized by spasms of actual physical pain.

He was thankful when a voice behind him shook him from his disturbing reverie.

"There you are, son," John called out. "How did it go?"

"Mr. O'Malley works well enough on the cross-country," Eric said. "I'm not too pleased on dressage, though. His movements aren't nearly precise enough."

"That's Hope's fault. She let him get away with murder."

"I figured as much. If he weren't so tractable, I'd have a real fight on my hands."

"You used the French snaffle?"

Eric nodded. "He doesn't take to the other bits, but that one seemed to help."

"Too bad women aren't as easy to tame, eh?"

From the mischievous look on John's face, Eric had to assume he was referring to his latest noticeable tiff with Mary. "The girl is a tough one."

"Some are." John smiled. "My Katie was—is—a real spitfire sometimes. Makes for an interesting life."

"At least Katie likes you."

The older man laughed. "I'd have thought, from the looks of you, you'd be able to handle women."

Eric snorted. "Women, yes. Mary Mulraney... well..."

"Ah, yes. Motherhood has changed her."

"I know."

Lost in thought, Eric looked once again toward the driveway. Still no sign of her. It was then that he fully realized how revealing his slip of the tongue might be and turned his full attention back to Day. The man was nodding.

"Something told me you probably did," John remarked offhandedly. "My sister and her husband carted that poor child all over hell, chasing trophies. You two were bound to have met, back in the old days."

"Once or twice," Eric said, glad to have been offered an easy opportunity to cover his mistake.

"How did she seem then?"

Giving the query some thought, Eric was surprised how much unhappiness he did recall. "She was lonely, I guess. Never had many real friends. Her parents kept her too busy for much of a social life."

"She's not lonely anymore," John volunteered. "She's not only got me and Katie, she's got her daughter." He paused. "Makes you see, doesn't it, why she'd hang on tight to the girl the way she does."

"Hope is her answer to the memory of being so alone?"

"That's my theory." He clapped Eric on the back. "But enough of that. How about a drink at O'Malley's? I could use a bite of pub grub, too."

Eric cast a glance at the road. "Shouldn't we wait for the women?"

"Ah, didn't I tell you? Katie telephoned. They've walked their feet off and taken a suite at the Shelbourne for the night." He chuckled. "That's their way of getting back at us, I'll wager. Katie knows I'll miss her cooking tonight and she's also picked the most expensive hotel she could find."

John steered Eric toward the stables. "Come on. Let's go get Will and bend an elbow together."

"I owe Will a round, anyway," Eric said. "I don't mean to offend, but I'll be drinking something a little less potent, if you don't mind. The ale over here hits me like the kick of a mule."

John guffawed. "If you want to stay on Will's good side, I don't think I'd mention that you don't like our brew. He practically lives on the stuff."

"It doesn't seem to affect him much," Eric said. They'd reached the far end of the stone wall that fronted the stable.

"As long as we walk home, I really don't care," John countered. "No drivin', though I don't mind if we crawl a bit."

"Who's crawlin'?" Will called out. He approached with a smile.

"You are, you old sot."

"Not yet, I'm not." His crooked grin broadened. "Do I smell the makin's of a party?"

"Just men," Eric told him. "All the women stayed in Dublin for the night."

Will chortled. "Good. They're more trouble than they're worth, anyhow." He fell into step beside the other two. "A' course, oul Eric here, he fancies young Mary." Will winked at John. "You and I are too far past it to care, aren't we, Mr. John?"

"Speak for yourself, Will Murphy. And I'll thank you not to embarrass our guest."

"Eric? Naw. He's no guest. Not anymore. If you ask me, he's family."

The words were spoken half in jest, yet Eric found the sentiment touching. If the hard-edged old groom could accept him, why was Mary fighting it so strongly? Later, if and when the time seemed right, he decided he'd ask one or both of his companions what they thought about the situation. After all, they'd known Mary and her family a lot longer than he had. If there was any clue, any help at all to be had from them, he intended to latch on to it.

One day without her had shown him more than all the previous time he'd spent having her near. It wasn't merely a matter of desire, like a craving for chocolate or an urge to race a fine horse over a tricky course. He needed Mary like the earth needed the sun, like fish needed water, like a man needed air to breathe. Without it—without her—he felt like he'd wither and die.

Mary had been to the Shelbourne once before, when Katie had spirited her away from the farm for a woman-to-woman getaway. In the last stages of pregnancy at the time, and still afraid she didn't really fit in at the Day farm, she'd not fully appreciated the hotel's nineteenth-century charm and beauty. Now, she did.

Hope's loud, "Wow!" echoed across the wide lobby and bounced off the crystal chandeliers.

"Hush." Stifling a laugh, Mary leaned down. "This is not the barn, Hope. Please, act like a lady."

"How?"

Mary cupped the upturned face in her hands. "Watch me and your aunt Katie, be quiet and no running in the halls. Okay?"

"Okay." She took her mother's hand and let herself be led passively to the elevator.

"This is a lift," Mary explained, a little concerned when the child hung back. "It's fun. You'll see."

By the time they'd reached their floor, Hope was grinning and Mary was thinking about all the other wonders the little girl had never experienced because she'd kept her so closely cloistered. That realization made the upcoming trip to Calgary even more of a treat.

Not that she intended to let herself get too excited about the prospect. It was enough to know that Hope would be exposed to life outside of the narrow world she'd known so far. Someday, when she was a little older, maybe they'd travel around Europe, just the two of them. It was an idea worth considering.

The bellman deposited their packages on the table and took his leave. Hope looked to her mother. "Can I talk now?"

Mary and Katie both laughed. "Yes," Mary said. "But no screeching."

The wide-eyed child made her way around the spacious, opulent room, touching everything and making surprised and pleased sounds. When she came to the painting above the heads of the beds, she stopped, her mouth dropping open, and pointed.

"Look! That horse is the same color as Mr. O'Malley. And see the people?" She began to grin and jump up and down. "There's me and Mama and Eric, too."

In the softly shaded landscape painting, a family sat in a flower-strewn field, having a picnic, their horse and cart nearby, their faces filled with love. And in that make-believe family, Hope saw Eric. Mary's eyes filled with unshed tears and she turned away to stare, unseeing, out the window at the spacious lawns and neatly tended flower beds of St. Stephen's Green that lay below.

The child grasped Mary's hand, drawing her back to face the painting. "See? I told you." Again, she pointed. "The little one is me and the mama is you and there's Eric. Right there.''

It *did* look like him, Mary thought.

"Was my real papa like him?" Hope asked.

So many months had passed since her daughter had brought up the subject of her missing father's identity, Mary had assumed she'd been satisfied with the patent answers she'd been given. Apparently, that was not the case.

"Your father was very handsome," Mary said, repeating what she'd often told the curious child.

"But could he ride? Like you and me? Like Eric?"

"Yes," Mary said. "Very well."

"I knew it!" Hope danced around the room, spinning in happy circles. "Can I take my shoes off? This carpet feels sooo soft."

"Of course." Going about the business of locating their new nightgowns amid the scattered packages, Mary busied her hands to try and quiet her unsettled thoughts. Whether or not she should have told Hope the truth about her father from the start, the deed was done. As quickly as the child had changed the subject, Mary doubted there was anything to worry about. Her juvenile concentration was too short-lived to make any kind of sensible deductions equating Eric Lambert with the father she'd never known.

"You never told me that," Katie remarked, her eyes fixed on the dress she was hanging in the spacious closet.

Mary started. "Told you what?" She could only listen to her heart pound and pray her aunt didn't mean what she thought she meant.

"About your late husband. I didn't know he was a rider, too."

"Not like I was," Mary hedged, carefully choosing her words so she wouldn't have to actually lie. It was the truth. Eric wasn't like her; he was better.

"Oh."

"I'd rather not talk about him, if you don't mind," Mary said.

"Of course. We're here to have fun. I'm sorry. Let's get dressed and go down to dinner." Katie primped in the gilt-edged mirror over the nineteenth-century writing desk. "While we're in town, I believe I'll have my hair done. Don't want my John trading me for some colleen."

Stepping up behind her, Mary gave her shoulders a squeeze. "There's no chance of that."

Katie's eyes held a mischief that belied her serious tone. "Don't know about that, now. Many's the man who's strayed for a younger woman. The urge just comes over them like a fairy curse."

Mary's laugh was heartfelt. "Not Uncle John. He's a rarity."

"Some are," Katie said, catching Mary's gaze in the mirror. "But they're few, that's a fact. When you see one, it's wise to grab him before some other woman does."

"Meaning?"

"Just blabbering. Old women are allowed to do that, you know. It's expected of us."

"You think I should grab Eric, don't you?"

"Now, did I say that?"

"In your own way, yes." Mary took a deep breath, held it for long seconds, then exhaled slowly. "It's not that simple, Katie."

"True love seldom is."

Mary's eyes widened. "Who said anything about love?" She didn't like the sly smile that lifted the corners of her aunt's mouth and deepened her laugh lines.

"Have it your way."

"My way?" Frustrated, Mary threw her hands into the air and began gesturing broadly. "My way? The man has got me so turned around I wouldn't know *my way* if I tripped over it.''

"Bothers you, does he?"

"Drives me crazy!" she admitted with no hesitation.

"Sounds like love to me." Katie dismissed her niece as she grabbed up a bag from Jorgensen's on Dawson Street. "I'll shower first, if you don't mind."

Mary stared after her. No way could Katie be right about her being in love with Eric Lambert. In love with his memory, maybe, but not with the man he was now. She chewed on her lower lip, thinking, wondering, picturing Eric in 1984, reviewing her life since then.

Celibacy had unhinged her. That was it. She'd read about such things; about how people's minds snapped when they foolishly denied their natural urges. Her urges had pretty much lain dormant until recently. Very recently. The trip to The Curragh on Eric's lap had been the first time in longer than she could remember when she'd actually wanted . . .

Muttering an oath, she stared at herself in the mirror. A nun without a habit, that's what she was. And that was how she'd stay.

Out of the corner of her eye she caught a slight movement. Hope! Dear Lord, she'd forgotten all about Hope. The child had overheard everything they'd said, including Katie's ridiculous assumptions about love.

"You're not to say anything about this to Eric, you hear?" Mary ordered.

The nod of Hope's head was so slight it was barely perceptible.

"Your Aunt Katie was just making jokes. Understand?"

Hope nodded again, signifying comprehension, but Mary had the niggling feeling that inside the child's mind the dangerous idea of a love affair between her mother and her new friend from the United States was taking root and growing.

That was all she needed, Mary grumbled to herself. Someone else to start telling her how she should live her life.

The loud singing in O'Malley's wasn't professional but Eric swore he'd never heard sweeter or more mellow ballads. And the food was tastier than anywhere else in the whole world. The strong brew grew on him, too.

He joined in another toast, the language of which he couldn't decipher, though it hardly mattered. To him, it was the belonging, the close-knit fellowship that was important. Coming into the pub between Will and John had made him an instant member of the unofficial club and he reveled in the camaraderie.

"Another round for all my friends," Eric said, raising his empty mug. "And be sure mine is still smilin'."

John laughed and thumped Will's shoulder. "Lord, he even sounds like the rest of us. We'll have him spoiled good in another hour or two."

"Aye." The groom chucked Eric on the arm. "I told you the Guinness would grow on you."

"It's delicious. Don't know why I didn't take to it right away."

"An acquired taste, it is," Will explained. "Just like fine Irish women. You learn to love 'em after a while."

"Women are too much trouble," Eric countered, noticing how unsteady his chair seemed all of a sudden. "Give me a wild horse with a burr under its saddle anytime."

Leaning closer, John whispered hoarsely, his voice carrying above the clamor and singing. "It's bred in us, you know."

"Loving horses?"

Eric's alcohol-induced innocence made John laugh. "Naw. Handlin' Irish women. It's a gift, passed down from father to son."

"My father was mostly German, I think," Eric said, wondering why his speech seemed a little slurred. He swore he hadn't drunk much.

"A pity." John quaffed the rest of his pint. "Barkeep! My glass has a hole in it."

Eric reached into his pocket to pay again, but John stopped him.

"You've bought enough rounds. The next six are on me."

"Six?" No way could they have polished off six apiece, he mused. Why, he would be drunk as a skunk if he'd done that. At least, he *thought* he would be. He'd never allowed himself to have more than two beers at a time, and then only when he wasn't due to ride, which was almost never, so he really couldn't be sure.

"Have another pickled egg or some more peanuts," John urged. "Got to keep your strength up for the war."

Eric was beginning to feel like a movie patron who'd walked into the theater halfway through the film and missed out on the entire plot. "War? What war?"

"The war of the sexes, son. Women don't know it, but we're the better sex. Always have been."

Chuckling, Eric pictured what Mary's reaction would be to a blatantly biased statement like that.

"What's so funny?" John leaned hard on the table.

"I was just thinkin' of Mary."

"Not surprisin', is it, Will?"

The old man shook his head. "Nope. I'd have bet she'd be the one."

Eric sat taller. "It's not like that."

"Like what?"

"Mary. Me and Mary. Oh, hell." He sipped his ale, the act leaving a foamy mustache on his upper lip.

"The boy's gettin' parletic, Will," John said. "Startin' to mumble about Mary."

"Like you said, it's not surprising." He leaned closer to his boss and drinking partner. "Think we ought to take him home?"

"Probably," John said, starting to rise. "Want to give me a hand?"

Eric felt himself drifting toward the door, one man on each side. Funny how muted the music had become. Obliging folk, these big Irish friends of his. He waved a bold farewell to the other pub patrons.

Outside, the cold, moist air hit him like an icy rag in his face. He shivered. "Jeez. Who put me in the deep freeze?"

"It's good for you," John told him sympathetically. "My guess is, you'll have one swelled head in the morning."

Eric leaned mostly against the shorter, stockier Will to keep his balance since John didn't seem to be any too steady himself.

"My Katie will be fit to be tied, that's a fact," John mumbled.

Will guffawed. "Katie, nothin'. I'm stayin' out of Mary's way for the next few days."

"Mary?" Eric knew someone had mentioned Mary but he wasn't quite sure who, or why. "Mary's so sweet," he slurred, "like honey."

"There's bees in honey, son," Will warned. "Ask any bear that's raided a honey tree."

"I didn't *mean* to," Eric said, growing instantly depressed. "She was just so pretty and so sexy and it was over before I . . ." He realized how telling his words were. "Oh, damn." Looking from John to Will, he expected them to order him drawn and quartered by the nearest team of horses. Instead, his guilty gaze was met with ones of compassionate understanding.

"We figured there was more between you and Mary than she wanted known, especially when she wouldn't watch your part of the competition on television a while back," John said. "Hell, she practically ran out of the room." Slowly getting control of the muscles in his arm, he patted Eric on the back. "I can understand why she'd act so embarrassed and want to hide how she felt, for Hope's sake, but why did it take you so long to own up to bein' a father?"

"I didn't have any idea what had come of our... you know... till a few days ago," Eric explained. "If you hadn't invited me over here, I still wouldn't know about the girl. Mary never let on." He noticed Will's nod.

"Told you, Mr. John. This here's an honorable man."

"You plan to marry her now?" John asked.

Managing to stand clear of the two, Eric drew himself up tall. "Not unless that's what Mary wants. If it helps any, I do love her, but you've got to let me handle this my way." In the looks they exchanged, he saw agreement.

"Does Hope know you're her father?" John asked.

Eric's heart began to race. The more people who were privy to the truth, the more likely a slipup. "No! And she mustn't. Not till Mary sees fit to tell her. I gave my word." The moisture that gathered in his eyes surprised him. He hadn't felt so much like weeping since he was a little boy.

He leaned back against a tree and stared up at the moon, which was encircled by an orange halo of mist. "Oh, God. If Mary knew I'd had too much to drink and let on to you two about our past, she'd never speak to me again."

John extended his hand. "A pact, then. We'll swear."

"You'd do that? For me?" Eric was overcome, his defenses sorely weakened by the excess alcohol in his system.

"Aye." Will joined John. "We swear."

As Eric placed his hand on theirs he wondered if there was any concrete truth to the legend of gold at the end of the rainbow or if the tales referred, instead, to the priceless gold of this kind of friendship, the likes of which he'd never imagined before tonight.

Chapter Nine

Mary sensed that Will was avoiding her and had been since she'd gotten home from Dublin. Not that she minded. There were times when the old curmudgeon could be awfully trying, especially when he took a notion to meddle in her affairs, which seemed to be most of the time as of late.

At least Hope seemed content, Mary thought thankfully. All Katie's foolish talk about love and Eric apparently had less effect on the child's creative imagination than she'd expected. Good. The next few weeks promised to be difficult enough without Hope playing matchmaker.

Mary spied Eric across the stable yard. A warm affection spread within her, intensifying in the apex of her soul, the place she'd kept sealed off for so long. She tensed. It wasn't really love she was feeling. Katie had been wrong about that. The word *admiration* fit pretty well. So did *pride*. Mary was proud of the worldwide fame and accomplishments of Hope's father. But she didn't love him. The love she'd once nurtured had faded and died long ago, leaving a wake of fond remembrances tinged with unbearable pain. It was a recurrence of that pain she wanted no part of.

Happily, Eric also seemed distant today. According to Katie, John was nursing a hangover he'd gotten when he'd taken Eric and Will to O'Malley's for their evening meal. Chances were, Eric was in no better shape than John. She chuckled to herself. It served them right if their heads ached. Her idea of a celebration was a hot fudge sundae with whipped cream or half a bag of chocolate-chip cookies, so she had little empathy for those who drowned themselves in ale and called it fun.

Katie had already delivered a pot of soup to Mary's for dinner and had suggested, in deference to John's pounding head, that they skip the usual gathering in the main house. Mary breathed a sigh of relief. This was one night she wouldn't have to sit across from Eric and try to make polite conversation while her stomach churned and her hands trembled.

Having lost interest in hanging around the stables since Mr. O'Malley was no longer hers to command, Hope joined Mary on the walk home.

"Eric has a bad headache today, so he only rode for an hour," the little girl said.

Controlling her smile, Mary nodded sagely. "I see."

"Don't you think we should ask him for supper, since Aunt Katie isn't cooking, tonight?"

"No, I don't." Mary glanced sideways at her.

"Oh."

"Katie sent a kettle of soup for our dinner. I'm sure she's provided well for Eric, too."

"How do you know?"

"Because your Aunt Katie is a considerate person. She wouldn't let her guest go hungry just because Uncle John is sick."

"That's good, huh?"

"That Uncle John is sick?" Sometimes Mary had a devil of a time following the youngster's convoluted train of thought.

"No, silly. To feed people. You know, like you said."

"Oh, to be considerate of others? Of course it's good." The wide, satisfied grin that Hope flashed made Mary's stomach lurch.

"Good," the little girl said, "because I invited Eric to our house to eat, just like Aunt Katie would do."

"Ho-o-pe..." Mary drew the name out slowly. "Are you playing games with me?"

Innocence shone in the clear green eyes. "No, Mama. He just looked so sad I felt sorry for him."

"Sad? Why?" With everything going his way, she couldn't imagine he'd be unhappy. Hung over, maybe. Sad, no way. Hope had to be mistaken.

Hope skipped on ahead and opened their front door. "Because he has to leave tomorrow, silly."

"He's leaving tomorrow?" Mary barely noticed the slamming of the door behind her, her pulse was hammering so loudly in her ears. "Did he say why he was leaving?"

"Uh-huh. Mr. O'Malley is really bad when I'm around and Eric thinks he'll learn better if he takes him away from here to train him."

The decision made perfect sense. What confused Mary was her reluctance to see Eric go. What was the matter with her? For days she'd prayed he'd leave and let her get back to the quiet, uneventful existence she'd been leading. Now that he was really going, she should be overjoyed. The trouble was, she felt the opposite.

"Dinner?" she repeated, the concept finally sinking in. "You asked him for dinner?"

"Uh-huh."

"Did he accept?"

The child looked puzzled. "'Course. Why wouldn't he?"

Mary glanced around the room. Newspapers were scattered on the couch, some of their recent purchases still lay in bags on the table, and someone had tracked mud across the colorful braided rug, all the way from the front door to the kitchen.

"Never mind," Mary said. "Just tell me what time you told him to be here."

Hope looked chagrined. "Time? No time. I just asked him to come."

"Terrific." She took the child's hand. "In that case, you get to help. Put your new clothes in your room, then run the vacuum while I dust. And see you don't bump the chair legs this time."

"But—"

"No arguments." Mary faced her sternly. "You asked him and you'll help me get this place ready for company."

"I should go tell Mr. O'Malley goodbye," she countered, starting to pucker up.

"No tears, either. It won't work this time," Mary said, her no-nonsense tone confirming her stance. "After we've eaten, we'll all go up to the stables and see Mr. O'Malley."

Hope brightened. "All of us?"

No doubt about it, the kid had her cornered. Too bad she didn't listen to details that closely all the time. "Okay. All of us. Now get a move on. We don't want Mr. Lambert thinking we keep a dirty house, now do we?"

"No, ma'am."

While Hope ran to do as she was told, Mary gathered up the stack of newspapers, hugged it to her chest and looked at her living room with a critical eye. It was undoubtedly homespun and informal beyond anything Eric or his well-to-do family had ever had. He'd probably think her home was totally unrefined and far too casual when he saw how she'd decorated the place. Mary sighed. That was just as well. The sooner he realized how different they were, how disparate their lives had become, the sooner he'd give up trying to get to Hope through her and accept the familial relationship on the terms she'd set forth.

Tossing the papers into the trash, she hurried to the kitchen to warm the soup and make a pan of soda bread. Leaving. Eric was leaving. The thought just kept running through her head like an unforgettable tune. No matter how hard she tried, she couldn't convince herself to answer, "Good riddance." In spite of all the upheaval he'd caused, she was going to miss him.

"She went home?" Eric asked Will. There was no need to specify who "she" was. A man didn't often shave, comb his hair and change to his best clothes to impress a seven-year-old. They both knew it was Mary he meant.

"Aye." The groom looked him up and down. "Has she agreed to start seein' you?"

Eric shook his head and sighed. "No. This was Hope's idea. I'm supposed to come to dinner."

"Ah. A smart girl, that one. Knows what needs to be done. You should be proud."

"Hush." He held up his hands to Will in supplication. "You promised."

"I know, I know. But there's no one close by and the truth's the truth. It's proud you should be."

Eric smiled. "I am. Have been since before I figured it all out. I'd expected Mary's daughter to be a wonder, but the child is even more talented than I'd thought when I first saw her." He frowned as his smile faded. "I saw her jump the lane, Will. It scared me good."

"She's a wild one, that's the truth."

"So, what am I going to do about it?" Eric ran his fingers through his hair. "If I'm not here, who'll make sure she's safe?"

"Mary's done pretty well so far."

"Except for discipline," Eric countered. "No parent should put up with such blatant disobedience, especially when it can result in injury or even death." He muttered oaths and paced away for a few seconds before going on. "Hell, Will, Hope is too precious to take chances with, yet if I insist that Mary let me help correct her, she'll think I'm trying to usurp her power as a parent."

"Aren't you?"

Snorting derisively, Eric nodded. "Yes, I guess I am. But it's not for me, it's for Hope. She needs a firm hand."

"Maybe her mother does, too," the old man suggested.

Eric softened. "No. I don't want to break Mary's spirit, I just want her to let me back into her life."

"For the girl?"

"For all of us," Eric said quietly, seriously. "I think we need each other. I know I need the two of them."

"Have you told her?"

"No." Eric began to pace anew. "I tried, a couple of times, but the words came out wrong and Mary got the idea that I wanted to get close to her so I could steal Hope's affections. I can't seem to make Mary see that I really do care about her, too."

"Maybe, in time..."

"I have high hopes that when we get to Calgary, I can make her understand my motives aren't bad ones." He turned to stare down the lane toward the cottage. "She's gone home, you say?"

"Aye. The girl's with her."

Eric straightened his jacket and squared his shoulders. "In that case, I'd better get over there before Mary thinks of an excuse to cancel Hope's invitation."

"I don't think she'd do that if she could," Will offered.

Pausing, Eric looked back at him. "You don't? Why not?"

"I just don't." Will pulled on the brim of his cap to settle it lower over his forehead. "You might be real surprised if you could see into that head of hers."

"It's her heart I need to see into," Eric countered. "And I think before she'll let me do that, she's going to have to be brave enough to take a good, long look herself."

"There's a bit of the poet in you," Will said. "You'll make the lass a fine husband."

"Hah! That could take a miracle."

The groom chuckled. "That it could. But in this land, I think you'll find that's what we do best."

Mary wasn't ready when Eric knocked at her door. She wouldn't have been any more ready if he'd taken a month or even a year to arrive. She'd never be prepared for the unsettling things his presence did to her equilibrium or the scary thoughts he brought to mind with one languid smile. And his touch...oh, dear.

Trembling, she grasped the knob, consciously pasted a smile on her face and opened the door. What she saw took her breath away. Not only was Eric as handsome as ever, he'd added an element she wasn't ready for—humility. Beneath his ever-present strength of character and directness of purpose, she glimpsed the boy she'd once loved, in all his youthful vigor and unpolished innocence.

Eric smiled down at her. She was breathless, as if she'd run to answer his knock. How he wished her excitement could be attributed to a more personal cause. Her cheeks were flushed, her eyes bright, her hair slightly windblown-looking, and he found his urge to sweep her up into a bone-crushing embrace almost too strong to subdue.

"Hi." Brilliant opening line, he thought. How profound. Such a way with words. Will should hear him now. Poet. Hah!

"Hi." Mary moved aside to admit him. "Hope said you were coming."

"You don't mind?" Eric immediately cursed himself for providing a chance for her to tell him she did, indeed, mind. To his intense relief, she said nothing.

He stepped into the room. Open beams arched across the ceiling to a stone fireplace where a blazing fire radiated a warm glow that encompassed the whole room. On the floor, a hand-braided rug led his eye to the sofa and antique rocking chair. On both, colorful pillows beckoned the weary to rest. Eric looked around, taking it all in, and found he was speechless.

"There. Now you've seen how we live," Mary said, her voice reflecting her tension.

"I wouldn't have believed any place could feel so good," he told her, still staring at the homey room. "How did you do this?" He strode to the fire and let his fingers trace the old stones in the hearth. "It's wonderful."

"What? You like it? I thought...well, you do come from a wealthy family and I supposed..."

"That I'd be stuck up? Spoiled by affluence?" He laughed, his chuckle adding to the already cordial atmosphere the room itself generated. "It takes more than money to make a home, Mary. You of all people should know that."

Chagrined, she agreed. "You're right. I was selling you short. I'm sorry." Her lips lifted in a genuine grin. "So, you really like it? I put it all together myself."

"You're an artist," he said simply. "Have you ever considered taking up decorating?"

"For other people? No. This house was a labor of love. It's special. I don't know that I could do it again and have it come out as well." She grinned more widely. "You really *do* like it, don't you?"

He approached, taking her hands tenderly into his. "Yes. Maybe it's the love you spoke of that I feel here."

Panic filled Mary. The look in Eric's eyes was melting her as surely as the fire in the fireplace would make short work of a block of ice. Was that what she was? she wondered. Was she ice to his fire? Or were they both fire, which, once joined, would burn out of control? She couldn't afford to find out.

"I don't want to hear how you feel," Mary said, pulling away from him. "My daughter invited you without asking me first, but because I've tried to teach her good manners, I'll honor the invitation." It was a self-protective exaggeration and she was instantly sorry she'd been so blunt and thoughtless when she saw how her words had cut him.

"I can go," he offered quietly.

The timbre of his voice sent shivers racing along her spine. From the look on his face, she could tell he meant every word. He would leave. All she had to do was tell him to. But she couldn't.

"No." The gentle persuasion in her voice was greater than she'd intended it to be. With that one word, she feared she had let Eric know how much she desired him, how much she wanted him to stay.

He paused, studying her, then stepped back to give her space. "Thank you."

Once again, he touched her soul. In his eyes, she saw true gratitude, poignancy far beyond what would be expected with the familiar response. If they continued as they had been, she knew she'd be in his arms, her lips searching for his, in a matter of moments.

Desperate, Mary did the only thing she could think of to break the spell. She called to Hope.

The little girl dashed into the room and launched herself at him. "Eric! You came!"

Bending down, he caught her up in his arms and swung her around. "Hello, champ. I'm going to miss you. Remember, you promised to do as your mother says while I'm gone."

Hope drew an imaginary X across her chest. "I swear. No more jumping and no more riding alone." For a moment, the enormity of her promise seemed to lower her spirits, then she grew bubbly again. "Eric's gonna teach Mr. O'Malley dressage, Mama. And he says he knows about a mare that would be perfect for me."

Mary cocked one eyebrow, her tender feelings for Eric rapidly dissipating. "Oh?"

"Uh-huh. She's kind of silver-colored. He says she's the best one for me because she's small and I could even ride her in shows someday, if I wanted."

Mary folded her arms across her chest. "We don't have a mare like that."

Eric looked her straight in the eye, his gaze unflinching. "No, but I do. There's a Dutch Warmblood I've been saving for just such a rider. She's gentle and surefooted." He paused, staring hard at Mary. "And she won't take a jump that's not safe. Not even if her rider insists." A quick glance at Hope emphasized his point. "The horse won't let an eager little girl push her too far and get them both into trouble."

"Hope can ride our horses," Mary insisted. "There's no need for you to go to all that unnecessary trouble."

"It isn't unnecessary trouble if it saves her from serious injury," he countered. "I know Hope means well but how long do you think it will be before her spirit gets the better of her and she's jumping again? Without O'Malley to look after her, who knows what trouble she'll get into?"

Mary gathered the child close to her side. "Hope won't jump if she's promised you she won't. We Mulraneys keep our word."

"I keep mine, too," Eric said. "And I promised the child the use of the mare. I've had my assistant in the States make sure the horse has the required vaccinations and vet certification for shipping. She'll be the first exchange of bloodlines between John and me."

"Excuse me," Mary said, trying her best to hold her temper. "I *am* Hope's mother. You should have consulted me."

"And I'm . . ." Eric squelched the rest of his reply. "As soon as Hope no longer needs an equine baby-sitter, the mare will be used for breeding. In the meantime, I trust you'll permit her to ride it." He paused, his jaw muscles clenching. "Please?"

Mary was no fool. She knew her daughter was unhurt only because of a kind Providence and overworked guardian angels. Eric was right. A more docile horse would help, as would getting Mr. O'Malley away from her.

Looking at the situation from a different angle shook Mary's confidence in the validity of her assumptions about Eric's ulterior motives regarding Mr. O'Malley. Could it be that Eric had wanted to eliminate the risk to his daughter by usurping the use of the spirited horse and taking it to Canada? That idea had not occurred to Mary before and its significance weighed heavily on her already overburdened conscience.

She looked into Eric's eyes and saw his open concern. That *was* what he'd done. "All right," she said. "I hate to admit it, but I do trust your judgment."

Once again, his soft, honest "Thank you" raced along Mary's nerves, straight to her heart. He did love Hope. If there were a way to accurately gauge such ethereal things, she imagined she'd find that Eric's love was nearly equal to her own. In a world where so many children knew no such love, she could hardly begrudge Hope the extra measure from her father, especially since it was so obviously genuine.

Mary's heart lurched. She excused herself and fled to the kitchen to finish preparing their meal. A few minutes alone and she'd be fine. All she needed was a distraction, a chance to recoup her self-assurance and calm her nerves by going about the mundane tasks of daily living.

She sensed, rather than saw, Eric come up behind her. When he spoke, she stood very still, averting her face. To look at him would be too heartrending. Already, tears were pooling in her eyes. She would not shed them. Not in front of him. Not because of him.

He gently grasped her upper arms. "I did it again, didn't I?" he asked sadly.

"I don't know what—"

"Took your authority without thinking." His fingers massaged her upper arms through the soft wool of her sweater. "I am sorry, Mary. This parenthood thing is all so new to me, I'm afraid I'm handling it poorly."

Stirring the soup kettle, she sighed. "It'll be all right."

"You mean, I'll learn?" Eric felt her stiffen within his grasp and released her, stepping back.

"No," she said, still refusing to look at him. "I mean it will be all right again once you've gone."

"That's tomorrow."

She answered with "I know," so softly it was almost a whisper.

Chapter Ten

Mary tried her best all evening to ignore the fact that Eric seemed to fit into her house as if he'd always lived there. His presence caused her to remain in a state of constant agitation, it was true, yet at the same time he brought a comfort that added depth to the peace she usually enjoyed. Remembering that he'd be leaving the following day allowed her to relax enough to thoroughly enjoy their meal.

"Aunt Katie made the soup," Hope had informed Eric when he'd complimented Mary on the food, and Mary had been able to laugh with genuine good spirits at the perplexed look on his face.

It was a dear face, in spite of everything, she finally admitted to herself. And although it seemed she'd made a habit of trampling all over his feelings, she really didn't mean to. She likened herself to a mare whose foal had been threatened. Dealing with the threat was of primary importance. Later, when things had settled down, she'd sort out her motives.

"I can make more coffee and we can have cookies for dessert," Mary offered. "I'm afraid that's the best I can do on such short notice."

Eric leaned back and rubbed his stomach before stretching lazily. "Peanut-butter cookies?" He held up his thumb and forefinger. "About this big around and this thick?"

"Yes. How did you know?" His sheepish grin focused on Mary, then passed to Hope before he turned his attention back to the girl's mother. "How long has it been since you checked the contents of your cookie jar?"

Judging from the lopsided smile he'd bestowed on Hope, Mary had a pretty good idea what had happened. She studied the child's lowered lashes, her flushed cheeks. "You took a treat with you to the stables today?"

Hope nodded rapidly. "You said I could."

"I said you could have a few cookies."

Coming to his daughter's rescue, Eric spoke up. "I had my dessert early, that's all. The cookies were good—at least, the first eight or ten were."

Mary mouthed "eight or ten" at him and watched astounded while he affirmed the numbers.

"Of course, that doesn't count the one I saw her slip to Mr. O'Malley or the ones that fell apart in her pockets." He grinned over at Mary. "To tell you the truth, I'm not sure how many I ate. They were mostly crumbs and lint, toward the end."

"Oh, yuck." Mary left the table, returning seconds later empty-handed. "Sorry. She got them all. I'll make another batch." She'd started to say "tomorrow," then realized Eric would be gone and stopped herself. In his eyes, she saw that his heart had clearly heard the word she'd held back.

He rose and started to pile his dishes. "Let me help you clean this up before I go."

"That's really not necessary. It's late and we don't want to keep you. I'll see to it in the morning." Mary looked over at Hope. "Time for bed."

The girl's eyes widened. "We haven't been to see Mr. O'Malley, like you said we would."

"Oh, darn." Mary had truly forgotten their earlier discussion. Of course, Hope remembered it perfectly. She would. With a deep sigh, Mary acknowledged that the child had a valid point. "You're right. I did promise." She turned to Eric. "We'll walk with you part way and tell Mr. O'Malley goodbye at the same time." It wasn't a perfect plan for getting Eric out of her kitchen and on his way, but it would do.

Eric made a disgusted noise. "Hope gets her way with you all the time, doesn't she? Do you ever actually discipline her? Children need rules, you know."

Mary wasn't about to stand there and take his criticism of her methods of child-rearing without rebuttal, especially since he was not in possession of all the facts. "They need fairness and understanding," she countered. "Something I got precious little of when I was growing up."

"You can't correct your upbringing by ruining Hope's."

"Ruining?" Mary couldn't believe her ears. How dare he! Eric lifted his shoulders in a heavy shrug. "Okay. Bad choice of words."

"I'll say." Mary looked at Hope. "Go get your coat."

Hope's resulting smile of triumph was as transparent as Eric's harsh assumptions had indicated it would be. Hope *was* manipulative, but then, didn't every child try the same tactics? Surely her daughter wasn't the only one good at it. She looked over at Eric, her eyebrows arched as if to ask his concurrence with her discovery. He scowled and nodded.

In the few minutes that Hope was out of the room, Mary managed a half smile for Eric's benefit. "Okay, so she's a little spoiled."

"Awfully."

"I suppose that comes from being around mostly adults all the time."

"And because her mother's tried to compensate for what she felt she missed as a child." He rested one hand lightly on Mary's shoulder.

"I'll get her squared away, Eric. Now that I'm aware there's a problem, I'll fix it."

"I know you will."

She stared at him. "No argument? You surprise me."

"No. No argument. You're an intelligent woman, Mary. All you needed was a push in the right direction and a more objective outlook." He smiled slightly. "You'll do fine. You're a good mother."

Mary could see that he meant every word, and the sentiment touched her profoundly. Maybe now he would back off and let her alone. Let Hope alone. If he was truly concerned only about his daughter's welfare, then he should be happy that everything promised to work out to his liking.

Hope returned at a run, still grinning. "I put my boots on, too, so I can brush Mr. O'Malley in his stall." She looked cautiously at Mary. "Okay?"

"That's fine." Mary reached for her coat. Taking it from her, Eric helped her into it. The gentle touch of his hands seemed to linger on her shoulders and she let herself rest against him for the briefest moment, drawing solace from his strength.

Had she known the simple act would so greatly magnify her need for him, her desire to be rocked in his arms, she never would have permitted herself the tiny slip of self-control. Now it was too late. Mary could only pray Eric hadn't noticed the same closeness she'd felt, hadn't responded to her careless sign of affection the same way he had when she'd ridden on his lap in the van.

She wouldn't look at him, she vowed. Then she wouldn't accidently glimpse the truth, whatever it was. She didn't want to know if he was emotionally affected or physically aroused, if he wanted her as much as she wanted him. Just thinking about the possibility made her palms sweat, her hands tremble once again.

Her fingers were so weak and shaky she had trouble turning the knob to open the front door. "Darn. This thing has a habit of sticking."

"I'll get it." Eric reached past to help. His lean body pressed against her for an instant. An instant of ecstasy. He did want her. Mary's head whipped around, her eyes searching for his, and their gazes locked, the truth so evident to them both that neither moved.

Finally, he turned the knob. Hope burst out the door and skipped down the walk, leaving Mary and Eric behind.

His fingers lifted to caress her cheek and his mouth softened. "I'm sorry. I can't help what you do to me. You're so beautiful."

"No, I'm not."

Smiling gently, he brushed a kiss across her forehead. "You're like an angel come to earth."

It was easy to reject the flowery compliment because it couldn't be true, and it was that assurance which helped her lighten the moment. Whatever good points she did have, they were dependent upon her skills as a horsewoman, not on her looks. That was the way it had always been and always would be.

"You're deluded by a moonlit night," she countered. "Fortunately for both of us, I'm still sane."

Eric smiled ruefully and released her. "That, Ms. Mulraney, is a dirty, rotten shame."

"Spoken like a true convert," she teased. "Tell me, how was your night out with the boys at O'Malley's?" The silly look on his face made her laugh.

"They drank me under the table. Not that I'm proud of it." He snorted. "I think I even remember joining in the singing."

"You? The very proper Eric Lambert? I don't believe it."

"Neither do I." Starting down the walk beside her, he took Mary's hand and was pleased that she permitted the contact. The need to touch her was so great it had to be answered before he pushed himself too far and lost the tenuous self-control that was holding him in check. If he let go of his inhibitions, grabbed her and kissed her now, as his body urged, he knew he might never be able to make amends. Going slowly was killing him, but he saw no other option except giving up, and he was too serious a competitor for that.

Mary looked up at him. "Eric?"

"Yes."

"I do like you. I know I sometimes don't act like it, but I am still your friend. I just wanted you to know that."

"I'm glad."

She squeezed his hand. "Feel free to visit us often. I want to do what's best for Hope, and I have to admit your influence has been good for her."

Emotion welled up inside him until he wasn't sure he dared speak. There was only one other thing Mary could have said that would have affected him more profoundly. She could have told him that she loved him.

"Mr. O'Malley's over here," Hope called. "Come on, Mama. Say goodbye."

Reluctantly, Mary released Eric's warm grip. They'd come the rest of the way in silence but their closeness had increased as much as if they'd professed undying friendship and she was loathe to break the contact.

She lifted her hand to scratch the big chestnut under his forelock. "You be good, Mr. O'Malley, you hear?"

"He will," Hope assured the adults. "He's promised. He'll win, too."

"That's a lot to ask of him without more training," Eric said. "I don't want you to be too disappointed if he's not first."

"He will be," the little girl insisted. "You'll see."

"Go get your step stool so you can reach," Mary said. "I'll take his blanket off. Give him a good rubdown and we'll wait out here for you till you're done."

Eric helped remove the blanket. As they started away, he took Mary's hand again.

She smiled up at him. "You don't expect to win, do you?"

"It's unlikely."

"Then, why go?"

"I've been in touch with my staff—I told you I'd called about the mare—and they tell me Dutchman's Pride is limping badly. He won't be joining us in Calgary. That leaves Mr. O'Malley or one of my other horses, and frankly, I think Mr. O'Malley's the better choice."

"You picked him to get him away from Hope, didn't you?" From the way Eric's eyes widened in the moonlight and his head jerked around, she knew she'd guessed right.

"How did you know?"

"I didn't, at first. I thought it was all just a big plot to get to Hope."

Eric swallowed hard. Was Mary ready for the unvarnished truth? He sure hoped so because he was about to reveal it. Squeezing her hands, he turned to face her. "I . . . it did start out that way." When she tried to pull away as he'd anticipated, he held her fast. "Wait. Listen to the whole story."

"No blarney," she warned.

"None. I swear." Leaning his head back for a second, he took a deep breath and continued. "I did try the horse to get Hope's attention and keep her grounded but it worked far better for me than I'd thought any novice animal would."

"Go on." Mary began to relax. Watching Eric, it was evident how hard it was for him to confess. Doing so was costing him dearly. She admired his courage.

"Then it occurred to me that if I took Mr. O'Malley to the Masters in Calgary, Hope might ask to go, too. The way she always twists you around her little finger, I guessed you'd let her."

"Were you figuring to take my place with her?" Mary asked, afraid the answer would be so honest she'd have to start building new walls between Eric and herself.

"No." His response was immediate and forceful. "No. I thought you'd do exactly what you did do—plan to go along."

"You *wanted* that? But I thought—"

"Yes," he said gently. "I wanted you to go, for all of us to be together."

Mary shivered. Oh, dear Lord. It wasn't only Hope he wanted, it was her, too! As impossible as it seemed, Eric meant to have them both. Or at least to gain control of Hope through her. He must think she was either a terrible fool or a love-starved spinster. Well, she was neither and she'd prove it.

She squared her shoulders. No matter how serious he was, she was not going to allow herself to be included in his plans. If he wanted to act the part of Hope's father, she'd let him because it was so evident the child could use someone with a more objective viewpoint, but Mary wasn't going to become a permanent fixture in his life. Not in any way. Once the events in Calgary were over, she was done traipsing all over the world. She'd had more than enough of the nomadic life-style as a girl.

"That was a dirty trick to pull on me," Mary said, "but it worked. This time." Her newfound feeling of strength and a solid footing made her smile. "And you showed me how Hope was manipulating me. For that I'm grateful. From now on, she won't be able to do it so easily, but then, neither will you."

Eric arched one eyebrow. "I think I may have done too good a job of enlightening you."

Her laughter was hollow and strained. The only way to fully regain her lost equilibrium was to bluntly remind herself of the past, and to remind him, too, just as explicitly. "You were always an excellent teacher, Mr. Lambert. Why, back in Los Angeles, you taught me how to stand on my own two feet against the world."

To her surprise, he merely nodded when she'd expected a rebuttal or at least some plausible excuse. "I was the slow learner," he said. "It took me a long time to realize what I'd thrown away."

"Funny. Being thrown away was exactly what it felt like." Mary started back toward the stable. She had to distance herself from the anguish she saw in his expression. "In case I don't talk to you again before you leave," she called back, "have a safe trip."

"Wait." He caught her arm and stopped her. "You won't change your mind about going to Canada, will you?"

This was the moment of truth and she faced it bravely. "No. I won't change my mind. There's a lot of the world Hope hasn't seen and I want to be there to share her discovery of it." She paused briefly before deciding to continue. A man as determined as Eric needed things spelled out clearly. "Hope and I are a team, a twosome. As long as we have each other, that's all we'll need to be happy."

He was shaking his head in the negative. "You're wrong, Mary. I only pray it isn't Hope who suffers when you catch on to that fact."

"Hope will never suffer at my hand, Eric. Never."

"Just like you never suffered because of your parents?"

Mary clenched her teeth. He really knew all her weak spots, didn't he? She stood rigidly and glared at him. In spite of his repeated suggestions to that effect, there was no possible comparison between her role as a parent and the way she'd been raised. None. She refused to dwell on the possibility.

But she did. That night and for days afterward.

Eric's transatlantic telephone call was unexpected. That he asked to speak only to Hope was an even bigger surprise. Mary tried not to listen but couldn't help herself. She heard Hope's childish responses and noticed that the child asked no questions whatsoever.

When she hung up, Mary asked, "How's Mr. O'Malley?"

"Fine."

"The training is going well?"

"Uh-huh." Hope started for her room.

"How's everything else?"

"Like what?"

Why was it the girl chattered incessantly except when you wanted her to? "Like Eric," Mary finally forced herself to say. "How is he?"

"Fine, I guess."

"What do you mean, you guess?" Mary's heart sped. "Did he say something was wrong?"

"No."

"Well, what *did* he say?"

"Nothing much."

"Hope..." Mary drawled. "Talk to me."

"Well...I think he said he misses me."

Waiting, Mary bit her lip. "What else?"

"Oh, yeah. He misses you, too."

"Go on."

"That's all."

"You're sure?" The wide grin that spread across Hope's face reminded Mary of the look on the old barn cat the time it had made off with Will's lunch while he was busy, and had finally been cornered in an empty stall, halfway through the corned beef sandwich. Hope was definitely withholding something.

"Uh, well, I guess he did say to give you his love." She burst into giggles. "Love, ooh, icky stuff!"

Mary made a stern face and put her hands on her hips. "It's an expression, Hope. Like telling somebody to say hello to someone else. He didn't mean what you think."

"Yes he did."

"Oh, be sensible. Of course he didn't."

"Okay." The child approached and took her mother's hand. "Bend down."

When Mary complied, Hope plastered a wet kiss on her cheek. Smiling, Mary straightened. "What was that all about?"

The girl covered her mouth for a few moments while she giggled. "That was from Eric," she said. "He told me to kiss you for him."

Mary touched her cheek and thought of Eric's passionately intense kisses. She laughed to herself. The one she'd just received had lost *a lot* in the translation.

Chapter Eleven

Time that should have raced by, dragged interminably. It wasn't until they were flying over North America that Mary began to feel as if her life was finally back in motion.

She'd temporarily abandoned her quest to be the perfect, patient parent and changed seats with John in order to gain a brief respite from Hope's incessant chatter and questions. In spite of the aspirin she'd taken, her head still ached. It was throbbing worse than she'd imagined was possible by the time their flight landed in Calgary.

Mary rubbed her temples as she followed the rest of the passengers off the plane. If Eric was at the airport to greet them, as she suspected he would be, she didn't know what she was going to do, how she was going to behave. Part of her yearned to see him again, to hear his voice, while another part of her dreaded the encounter. All the mental rehearsals in the world were not enough to prepare her adequately for their meeting, and she knew it.

Hope saw him first, across the room, and let out her characteristic squeal of delight. Mary's head nearly split. She stared across the baggage-claim area with bleary eyes.

Roses. He was carrying a bouquet of deep crimson roses, wrapped in clear cellophane and tied with a red satin bow. If he thought a few flowers were going to make her fall into his arms and agree to become a part of the imaginary family he'd created out of some misplaced sense of duty, he was sadly mistaken.

What would be the best way to refuse the flowers? she wondered. Or should she simply accept them politely and not make a scene? In her present state of physical pain, she wasn't up to a fight, nor was she particularly eager to hurt his feelings. She just wanted him to understand she wasn't available, at least not to him. Someday, after Hope was grown, she might consider getting into a romantic relationship, but that day was a long way off, and besides, a world traveler like Eric Lambert wasn't the kind of man she'd consider, anyway.

Take the roses, her conscience ordered. What harm can a few flowers do?

Mary agreed. She had no desire to bruise his feelings or cause him unnecessary grief. Even if his motives were questionable, the gesture was a nice one.

Grinning broadly, Eric approached and shook John's outstretched hand. Mary held her purse and coat to her chest like a shield, waiting, finding herself breathless from the reaction his closeness brought. Maybe she wouldn't accept the roses, after all.

Practically ignoring Mary, Eric nodded a quick acknowledgment, then bent down to Hope.

"Hi, champ." Throwing her little arms around his neck, she hugged him fiercely. "Hey! Watch it," he cautioned with a laugh. "You're squashing your flowers."

"Mine?" Hope squeaked. "They're for me?"

"Of course they're for you," he said, presenting them with a flourish. "Who else would they be for?"

Who else, indeed, Mary thought, stopping herself just as she was about to make a sour face.

"For Mama."

"No," Eric explained. "This is your first trip out of Ireland and I wanted you to feel very special."

She took the bouquet. "I missed you, Eric. My new mare came after you left. She's pretty and she lets me ride without even a saddle. I named her 'Josophine.' I hope you don't mind."

He chuckled. "No, I don't mind. I think 'Her Majesty's Silver Fancy' was a bit too much name for her, anyway." He looked to John. "Without a saddle? Is that what she said?"

Mary found her voice and entered the conversation, uninvited. "That's what she said. She was brushing the mare on the second day we had her and decided she couldn't reach her long mane well enough, even with a step stool, so she climbed aboard. The rest is history. You should see them."

"I'm looking forward to it." He barely glanced at Mary before turning his attention back to Hope. "From now on, you're to always ride with a saddle. Do it correctly, okay?"

"That's what Uncle John said, too," Hope replied. "Josophine and I will be good, I promise."

He ruffled her curls as he stood. "Okay. Now let's get your baggage. I want John to see Mr. O'Malley work before the competition, day after tomorrow."

Hope tugged on his hand. "I want to see him, too!"

"You can watch us from a distance, if you promise to keep your voice down," Eric told her seriously. "I'm afraid if the horse knows you're here, he'll start to act up."

"Eric is right," Mary said, moving to the opposite side of Hope. "You and I will find a place to sit where Mr. O'Malley can't see us. After the competition, you can fuss over him all you want."

Hanging her head, Hope lagged back. "He'll know I'm there, anyway. He always could tell when I was coming."

Mary looked over the top of Hope's head at Eric, her nod answering his unspoken question. "The horse does seem to sense her presence."

"Then, do you suppose..."

"Yes." They'd stopped at the baggage carousel. No luggage from their flight had arrived yet. Mary bent down to look into Hope's face. "You want Mr. O'Malley to have the very best chance to win, don't you?"

"Uh-huh, but—"

"No," Mary said. "No buts. If our staying away is what it takes to give him that chance, then that's what we'll do. Eric is the boss." At least in this case, she added to herself.

Hope nodded a reluctant acceptance. "Okay." She pulled on Eric's hand, leading him a few steps away, where she motioned for him to lean down again.

Watching, Mary wondered what all the secrecy was about. She saw Eric smile and place a tender kiss on Hope's cheek before straightening. With dramatic seriousness, he studied the bouquet of roses, chose one and withdrew it carefully. Together, he and Hope rejoined Mary.

"She thinks you looked sad because you didn't get any flowers," he told Mary, "and she wants you to have one."

"Hope could have given it to me." Mary was not at all sure the decision had been arrived at exactly the way Eric had explained it.

His voice lowered, its resonance sending shivers up her spine. "That was what I told her. But she wanted it to come from me."

Mary put out her hand to accept the token gift. "What did *you* want, Eric?"

His fingers grazed hers and she flinched. The touch of his hand was as softly moving as the velvet of the rose petals. What had she been thinking? Her headache must have unhinged her. She should never have asked Eric such a leading question, not with Hope and John close enough to hear his response. He would probably make some rash statement that led them to suspect how much he wanted her and then she'd have to try to explain it all away when the only thing she really wanted to do was take another couple of aspirin and lie down.

"Me?" he said casually. "I hadn't given it much thought. I suppose if Hope wants to share her flowers, it's up to her." He moved away to help John with the bags.

Mary closed her fingers around the rose's stem and felt the prick of the thorns. The fleeting pain in her hand was nothing compared to the pain of experiencing Eric's offhand treatment of her question. Yet that was exactly the way she'd told him she wanted him to behave, wasn't it? They were to be friends, to share Hope in an informal way and to act as if there had never been anything special between them. She should know the rules—she'd made them.

So why did it hurt so much to see that in the time they'd been apart, Eric had come around to her way of thinking? Mary cringed inwardly. An honest answer to her question was too distressing to consider. Hope was happy. Eric was happy. So why was she feeling as if her whole world had just crashed down around her?

Their rooms at the hotel near the Spruce Meadows showjumping facility were adjoining, with two bedrooms and a separate sitting room, so that Hope could have her own private space and still be under Mary's care. Horse-oriented motifs and paintings of famous contenders were everywhere, including the bathrooms. The effect was pleasing but could certainly get to be overwhelming, should a person stay long, Mary mused. She shrugged. That wasn't going to be one of her problems. As soon as Mr. O'Malley had competed and the results were in, she was going back to Ireland.

Finishing dressing, she tucked the tail of her bright pink T-shirt into the waist of her white jeans. After the long flight she'd slept soundly, and this morning her headache was gone. Her heartache? Well, that was another matter.

Slipping a colorful, narrow headband over her hair to hold it away from her face, Mary went to the window. Summer in Calgary had always been pleasant in spite of occasional showers. Today was no exception. The morning sun sparkled on the man-made lakes of the resort and warmed the spruce and maple leaves that were just getting ready to turn to the reds and yellows of fall.

Horses were being exercised in the green field opposite her second-story window. Mary retrieved her binoculars from her suitcase and scanned the area. Mr. O'Malley wasn't among the magnificent mounts. Not finding him, she skimmed over the rest of the complement with true lack of interest. If Eric wasn't out there, what was the use of looking?

A knock on her door didn't surprise her. John was due to take them to breakfast and Hope had gone to fetch him. Mary had intended to locate Mr. O'Malley so she could placate the impatient child by pointing him out to her before they left the suite.

Determined to find the horse, she tried again as she called, "Come on in." Raising the field glasses, she peered through them. "I don't see him, Uncle John."

"You won't," the deep voice said smoothly. "He's in the barn."

"Eric!" Whirling, Mary tucked the glasses behind her.

"You don't have to hide your interest from me. I know you'd rather be in a box seat or at the fence, watching O'Malley." He didn't smile. "Speaking of which, where's Hope?"

"I sent her to get John. We're going to breakfast."

"And then what?" Leaning against the doorjamb, he made no effort to enter the room or to close the door.

"I don't know. Shopping or a museum, maybe. Anything to keep Hope from sneaking off to the stables and getting O'Malley all fired up for the wrong reason." Fired up like *she* got whenever Eric Lambert was close by, Mary acknowledged ruefully. Like every time she saw him. Like now.

"How about letting me take her to Heritage Park?" When Mary didn't answer, he expounded further. "The place in the center of the city? With the antique amusement-park rides? Remember? It had an old-fashioned city street and Victorian houses, and—"

"I remember," Mary snapped. "I remember, okay?"

Eric shrugged noncommittally. "I wasn't sure you'd recall having been there."

Not recall? How could she forget visiting Heritage Park with Eric, when the magic of their youthful adventure was still so fresh in her soul? Obviously, not as easily as he'd forgotten taking her there.

"I guess I saw it once—many years ago," she told him.

"So, do you want to tag along, too? I don't think Hope will mind, and you don't have too much else to do, unless you're planning on going down to the trade fair."

"No, not the fair. I'm afraid it would remind me too much of an unhappy part of my life just as well forgotten. If I go anywhere, it'll be to the Festival of Nations, later. I'd like Hope to see that."

Eric shrugged. "Fine. Then come along with us, for now. You said you wanted to help her discover the world." Feigning nonchalance, he held his breath and schooled his features into passivity. Do it, Mary, his thoughts urged. Come with me of your own free will. Give me a chance. Give us all a chance.

"It is a pretty day." Mary studied Eric's expression. Nothing in it reflected the turmoil she was feeling with regard to her memories of the park. If Eric didn't remember having been there with her, what was the harm in going? It was her past that lent such poignancy to the present. The fact that their time in Calgary had meant so little to him was a good sign. It reassured her that his current motives were as platonic as they seemed.

"Well?" he pressed. "Think of it as doing a public service. You can keep Hope from causing me trouble."

"What about Mr. O'Malley?"

"I've already worked him lightly for an hour this morning. The jumping events begin tomorrow. He should rest till then."

"I agree." She looked past Eric as Hope and John appeared in the hall behind him. "Uncle John! You can come along, too."

"Come where?" The older man paused to shake Eric's hand while Hope took the other.

"We were just talking about going over to Heritage Park," Eric told him, hoping the complacency in his voice wasn't so great that John would agree to accompany them. He liked the man, but it was Mary he wanted to be with. Hope was the catalyst needed to get Mary to go. John wasn't necessary. Eric looked him straight in the eye, sending signals of desperation and determination. Signals that were received.

"Sorry," John said. "I promised Mac and Virginia I'd meet them for lunch."

Mary drew a quick breath. "The Slones?"

"Yes." John smiled. "They said they remembered you. Maybe you'd like to join us."

"No, thank you. They were more Mother and Dad's friends than mine. I'd much rather spend my free time showing Hope the city."

Eric nodded to Mary, drew John into the hall and started to close the door. "Excuse us a minute, ladies." He smiled down at Hope. "Go ahead and get ready. We'll leave in a few minutes."

"Eric?" Mary knew there was a nervous edge to her voice but that couldn't be helped. If John got to blabbering too much to the Slones, or if they had heard even part of the sordid truth about her from her parents, the secrets surrounding Hope's birth would soon be common knowledge. She knew she shouldn't have left her sanctuary in Ireland.

Eric leaned through the narrowly open door. His tone was level, his demeanor unruffled. "I'll take care of it, Mary. Don't worry."

She trembled as he closed the door. How could he be so calm when his daughter was likely to soon become an object of censure? All the assurances in the world weren't enough to placate Mary. This might be the '90s, but John and Katie Day had always been terribly vocal in their views on the sanctity of marriage. If they found out about Hope, their gut reactions might very well hurt the child, even if they didn't mean them to.

Hope tugged on the pocket of Mary's jeans. "What's wrong, Mama? Don't you want to go to the park?"

Getting down on one knee, she took Hope's hands and smiled. "Nothing's wrong, honey. A trip to the park is a fine idea. I was just thinking about something else, that's all. We'll have a wonderful time today. You'll see."

Hope brightened. "Eric says there's a merry-go-round. I get to ride it."

"Yes. There is." She got to her feet so she could keep the child from seeing the tears that had suddenly misted her vision at the mention of the carousel. "Go get your sweater. It might be chilly."

Taking a drink of water, Mary used the time to collect her thoughts. What in the world was wrong with her? Strong reactions to constant tension were one thing, but her wild swings of emotion were beginning to try her patience. She certainly couldn't go through the entire day worrying about crying because of some stupidly sentimental old memories.

Nor was she willing to spend long hours alone in their suite, she decided easily. And she knew she didn't want to visit the show grounds with John. Not if the Slones were there. Not unless she was willing to put up with their reminiscences from her past for hours on end. Besides, if she were absent from whatever conversations they had with John, there was less likelihood they'd ask a lot of personal questions.

That left Heritage Park. And Eric. Mary managed a smile in spite of her concerns as she pictured the beautiful antique carousel. Remembering, she could almost hear the calliope music, see the platform revolving as a young man and a naive girl rode round and round, joking about a make-believe race aboard the wooden horses and laughing at the silly pretense. Until the day when she and Eric had finally consummated their love, that wonderful afternoon in the park had been the most cherished of her life. It was still number two on the list of all-time great occasions, she conceded. Maybe it always would be.

Standing tall, she squared her shoulders and made a conscious decision to dwell only in the present. What was past, was past. She'd made a whole new life for herself. With Eric around, it was too easy to forget that salient fact.

She looked hard at her image in the mirror over the sink, seeing the confident woman she had become. It took a strong person to do what she'd done so far—raise her child alone and make a good life for them both. Mary was no longer a lost, lonely child herself, and it would pay for her to remember that. She didn't need to lean on Eric—on anyone. Her own two feet were support enough. Survivors should never have to apologize for making it through terrible trials or for refusing to accept help that wasn't needed, or sought. She'd paid her dues. Membership in the human race didn't mean she couldn't stand alone if that was what she wanted to do.

Mary turned with a smile. "Grab a sweater for me, too, will you, Hope? I'll just put on some lipstick and I'll be ready."

"Okay."

"We'll have a great time," Mary said. A sidelong glance at Hope told her the little girl wasn't too sure about that. Mary went to her, accepted the sweater Hope had picked up and paused to look down at her. "What's wrong, honey?"

"Nothing."

Mary smiled gently. "Now, you sound just like me. Come on. Give. Why the long face?"

Hope shook her head, her eyes downcast.

Lifting her chin, Mary tried to guess what the problem might be. "You wanted Eric all to yourself today, didn't you?" The surprised look in the little girl's eyes confirmed her suspicions.

"It's okay," Hope said quietly.

"No, it isn't." Putting herself in Hope's place, she could see how much more exciting the outing would be for her without the usual authority figure going along to impose the rules. "Tell you what. Why don't we pretend Eric's your parent today, instead of me. I'll be the friend and you'll do as Eric says, instead of listening to me all the time. Then it'll be the same as if I'm not there. How does that sound?"

"Weird." Hope began to smile. "But fun."

"Good. Then suppose we go find him and get out of here before the whole day is wasted?"

Hope beat her to the door and jerked it open. Eric stood in the hall, still talking with John. They stopped when Hope dashed up with Mary close behind.

"We're almost ready," Eric said. His eyes telegraphed tranquillity and assurance that he'd prepared John without filling him in on too many details.

"I get to pretend you're the boss," Hope said, grasping his hand. "And Mama's just a friend, so I don't have to do anything she tells me. Isn't that neat?"

Mary blushed. Eric looked shell-shocked, but John had begun to chuckle. She tried to explain. "Hope didn't really want to be saddled with a nagging mother, so I transferred power to Eric, the way it would have been if I weren't going along." A smile of understanding lifted the corners of her mouth.

For a moment, Mary thought she glimpsed strong emotion in Eric's gaze, but when she studied his face further, there was no sign of anything except amiable acceptance of her plan.

"Then come on, champ," he said, starting off down the hall, "before she changes her mind."

Leaving John with a quick goodbye peck on his cheek, Mary hurried to catch up. "Not a chance, team. I'm in this for the duration. And I'll expect at least one ice-cream cone as a reward."

Hope giggled. Looking up at Eric, she beamed with pride and affection. "It's okay, then? You don't mind?"

"Being boss, or buying your mother an ice cream?"

"Being boss, silly."

"No, I don't mind. I like to tell other people what to do." With a grin, he shot a swift glance over his shoulder at Mary. "Everybody knows that."

"Can I call you Daddy?" Hope asked, her exuberance barely contained.

Mary butted in. "Hope, for heaven's sake. That wasn't what I meant." The charged look in Eric's eyes kept her from saying more.

"You mean, pretend I really am your daddy?" he asked the child quietly.

"Uh-huh. It would be fun."

"I think so, too." He turned to Mary for permission. "Is it all right with you?"

She cocked an eyebrow and nodded. At least he was learning to ask before acting. "What can I say? It was my idea."

Eric looked down at Hope. "Okay. It's a deal. But let's wait till we get to the park to start to play the game, shall we? The people I know at this show might get confused if you called me that name here."

"Okay." She skipped to keep up with his long strides. "I wish you really were my dad."

Mary held her breath, waiting for him to do the unthinkable and tell Hope the truth. Under similar circumstances, she wasn't sure she could have been as placid as Eric seemed to be. Instead of the revelation Mary's mind had envisioned, his response was simple and direct.

He smiled down at Hope and said, "I wish I was, too."

Chapter Twelve

Mary had forgotten that the park lay beside the Bow River. Boats of all descriptions bobbed along the dock and the entire lower parking lot seemed to be devoted solely to fishermen and their boat trailers.

Maneuvering the car he'd rented into the upper lot, Eric found an available parking space. "At least they drive on the right side of the road here," he remarked. "I wouldn't dare drive in Ireland till I got used to the opposite-side traffic."

"It did take time." Mary leaned forward to talk. She'd been relegated to the back seat, since she was the "guest." The official "family" seemed to be taking perverse pleasure in treating her like an outsider. Naturally, she hadn't objected. Being so near to Eric was hard enough without insisting they sit in closer proximity. The back seat was just peachy.

Trotting along behind, she followed Hope and Eric to the gates and let him get the tickets. Her heart did a flip-flop when she heard Hope's carefully pronounced "Thank you, Daddy."

"You're quite welcome, dearest daughter," he replied just as formally, grinning when Hope burst into a fit of giggling. He glanced at Mary. "Sounds just like her mother, doesn't she?"

"At times," Mary admitted. "Especially when her mother is feeling particularly keyed up." She pulled a face. "I like to think I've outgrown most of that foolishness."

"I hope not," Eric said, turning his attention back to Hope and giving Mary no opportunity for rebuttal. "So, champ. Where shall we go first?"

Hope's eyes widened. "The train! Look! It's so big."

"Okay. I'll race you." Eric was off down the grassy hill that sloped toward the tracks before Mary could speak. Not that those two would have listened to her anyway, she grumbled to herself. Eric was in the lead, acting just like a kid, and Hope galloped along behind, laughing and giggling as she gamboled with him in the bright sunshine.

Mary sighed. Oh, God. Just look at the two of them. What a picture they made. Father and daughter. Their joy radiated all around them, beckoning to her, showing her all too clearly what she was missing. Slinging her purse strap over her shoulder she started after them. No way were they going to run off and leave her. Why should they have all the fun?

She reached the tracks at a dead run, her momentum carrying her past the place where the others had stopped. Eric's hand shot out to grab her arm. Squealing, she slid to a faltering stop, but not before the force of her downhill plunge jerked him off his feet. They fell in a jumble of arms, legs and laughter while Hope stood off, hands on her hips, and shook her head at them as if they were misbehaving children and she were the parent.

"I told you I was too old for this kind of nonsense,"
Mary gasped out between giggles.

"Poor baby." Eric disentangled himself. Getting to his
feet, he held out his hand to Mary. "Are you really all
right?"

"Nope. My pride is mashed," she explained, dusting
herself off. The hand was still there, the help still offered.
Tossing caution aside, she grasped it and let Eric pull her to
her feet. His grip was warm, firm yet gentle, and it set off a
chain reaction in her body that threatened to knock her off
her feet again. She staggered. Instead of the added physical
support from him that she'd expected, he released her hand
and once more paid attention only to Hope.

"Come on, dearest daughter. Our clumsy friend is okay.
Let's go look inside the train."

Hope took his hand. "You can call me by my real name,
Daddy. It's okay not to call me 'dearest daughter.'"

She sounded so serious, Eric had to chuckle. "Oh, it is,
is it? Okay, Hope. But you keep calling me 'Daddy.' I like
the sound of it."

"You bet!"

Eric caught an image of Mary out of the corner of his eye.
She seemed to be all right. The beginning of his charge down
the hill had been a subconscious reaction, he supposed, because halfway down, he remembered holding Mary's hand
and doing the same childish thing a long time ago.

He snorted derisively. What a fool he'd been to think
she'd remember this place. Hell, she wasn't even sure if and
when she'd been here before. But *he* knew. Oh, yes, he
knew. It had all come rushing back to him when he'd started
thinking about Heritage Park, and the more he walked the
grounds, the more fond memories the experience triggered.

Like the carousel. They'd all go there last, he decided;
visit it as their final ride of the day. He wanted Mary to re-

member, to be able to reclaim some of the carefree youth she swore she'd abandoned forever. She needed to learn to have fun again. With him. For her sake and for Hope's, too.

He grimaced. All his motives weren't pure and altruistic. He wanted to go back to that summer when he and Mary had been friends and recreate a similar atmosphere so she could break the habit of always reacting to the past as if it had just happened without truly seeing how things had changed. How he had changed.

He held tight to Hope's hand as he helped her climb aboard the car behind the big, black steam engine. Mary was standing to one side, trying to brush grass stains off her jeans. His gut knotted as he relived the agony of relinquishing her touch when he'd helped her to her feet.

Eric knew what else he had to do. This entire day must be choreographed like a perfect dressage performance; each step just so, each signal barely perceptible, each response schooled and unperturbed. He'd learned the hard way that chasing after Mary was the wrong approach. She had to be made to see that the decision to commit to him was hers alone. Coercion wouldn't work. Neither would a strictly physical relationship. He'd let himself go too far with her once and possibly ruined three lives because of his lack of responsibility. He wouldn't make the same mistake twice.

Hope's call broke into his thoughts. "Daddy, can we ride this train? Really ride it?"

"Sure. If your mother wants to."

Pouting, Hope hung her head. "What if she doesn't? Can't we go without her?"

"No. We won't do that." Eric took one of her hands as he crouched in front of her. "I care very much for you, you know that, but I also like your mother. You're not in some kind of a contest with her to see who I'll like the most." From the disgruntled look on her face, he doubted he was making himself clear, so he tried again. "People like other people for themselves, just the way you like Mr. O'Malley and Josephine. They're both nice horses but they're not the same, so you love them for different reasons. See?"

"I guess so...Eric." Hope peeked past his shoulder at Mary, who waited below on the grassy slope.

No more "Daddy," he noted. Well, if that was the price he had to pay to eliminate the dissension between Hope and Mary, then he'd pay it, gladly. He hadn't intended to destroy their close relationship and he wouldn't press his case if he saw that was what was happening. The obvious love mother and daughter shared was too precious to jeopardize.

He stood and motioned to Mary. "The kid wants to ride. Come on."

"You go ahead," Mary countered. "I'll meet you back here."

"No way. I think I may need reinforcements. She's calling me Eric again."

Mary chuckled. "Uh-oh. That sounds bad."

"It is bad." He took her arm to help her. Hope had already run down the aisle of the car and was standing on the open rear platform, inside the iron railing. As soon as Mary was aboard, Eric backed off and pointed to the excited child. "She's a stubborn handful."

"You were the one telling me how to raise her a while back, so go ahead. Show me."

"Very funny." He made a wry face. "Besides, I'm new at this, remember?"

Mary looked around her to make sure they wouldn't be overheard. Another young couple with small children was close by, but between the groaning and huffing of the warming-up engine and the din of their own kids, they weren't likely to be able to hear what was being said, even if they tried.

She lightly touched Eric's arm to get his attention. "Which reminds me. What did you tell John about the Slones?"

"Just that they'd been serious rivals of yours and you'd rather not have them know about Hope till she was ready to compete against their son and beat the pants off him—figuratively, of course. John thought keeping our star pupil a secret would be a good joke on all the snobs who used to be so hard on you."

Mary's eyes widened. "You remember that?"

Had he said too much? He hoped not. "Sure. You used to tell me your troubles all the time. Kind of like I was your big brother."

That *was* how he'd often seemed, Mary recalled. To her, Eric had been father, friend, brother, confessor—everything. She swallowed past the dryness in her throat. Even lover. Especially lover.

She smiled shyly. "Did I ever thank you for listening?"

"I didn't do it for thanks," he told her offhand.

Mary held her breath, certain he was going to make a pass or at least say something overly familiar, something that would make her blood run hot in her veins. She needed the jolt of adrenaline his romantic advances gave her, needed it the same way a competitive rider needed the thrill of the race or the scare of almost missing a difficult jump. Such dangers made a person feel alive, vital, ready for anything.

When he didn't go on, she asked, "Then why did you listen to my troubles?"

He shrugged. "Beats me. Come on. The twerp is too far away to suit me. I want to keep my eye on her."

Watching Eric make his way up the narrow aisle of the antique, wooden passenger car, Mary wasn't sure whether

she wanted to run away from him for good or scream and
throw things. For a man who'd suggested they should become a family, he was sure acting as if he'd changed his
mind. Not that she wanted him to think she cared. She
didn't. Not really. It was just darned frustrating to be ready
to offer logical arguments against it and then have no opportunity to do so.

Scream and throw things, she decided. That was what she
felt like doing. She frowned. Lucky for Eric there·wasn't a
single loose object close at hand. Yes, sir. Lucky for him.
Grumbling to herself, she followed him up the aisle.

Eric had continued to be polite and to hold himself aloof
all day. Hope, on the other hand, had behaved so change-
ably and switched her loyalties between the two adults so
often that by evening Mary's patience was totally spent.

On the way home, the child had talked back to Mary, Eric
had reprimanded her, and she'd once again disowned him.
In the ensuing discussion, tempers had gotten so frayed
Mary wasn't sure whose point had triumphed, nor did she
care. All she wanted to do was flop down on the couch in her
suite and prop her feet up.

Following Hope into their rooms, Mary left the door open
and Eric entered, uninvited. She was too bushed to object.

"Oh, boy." Off came her shoes and headband. "Having
fun can be a bear."

"Especially when you take the cub along," he countered. "Where do you keep your aspirin?"

"In the overnight bag on the luggage rack. Bring me a
couple, too, will you?" She rubbed her toes through her
heavy socks. "Oooh."

"Where did Hope go?" Eric asked, delivering the bottle
of aspirin and going to the sink for glasses and water.

"She flounced into her room," Mary said. "With all the junk she ate today, I don't expect she'll want any dinner later, anyway."

"I don't suppose." He handed her a full glass of cold water.

"Mmm. Thanks." Mary noticed that he'd plopped down beside her, but after the trying day she'd had, primarily because of his disinterested demeanor, she wasn't concerned. Not that her body didn't care. Oh, no. It cared, all right, but the practical side of her had concluded that Eric Lambert had given up trying to sweet-talk or seduce her. It was a letdown, albeit a welcome one. Now, at least, she could relax around him without having to worry about being compromised. Darn it.

Opening the aspirin bottle, Eric shook out four tablets, two for each of them. "Here. *Bon appétit.*"

Mary chuckled. "Thanks. You too." By the time she'd swallowed her aspirin, Eric was already done and lying back against the couch with his eyes closed and his feet propped up on the coffee table. "Sore feet?" she asked.

"No kidding. We who ride for a living are not made to walk all day."

"We rode," Mary countered. "We must have stayed on that old merry-go-round through three cycles."

"Four." He opened his eyes only long enough to reach for her hand and draw it to his chest where he clasped it to him. "I had hoped..."

"What?" Mary studied his profile. He appeared to be at rest, but the pounding of his heart beneath her hand told another story.

"Nothing." His deep breath was almost a sigh.

Mary sat up straight and looked at him. The only indication he was even awake was the proprietary way he clutched her hand. "Tell me. What about the merry-go-round?" She saw his brows knit.

"It doesn't matter. Nothing does."

That kind of blanket statement wasn't at all like Eric, and his attitude worried her. A man who expected to win in a serious competition like the Masters the next day couldn't go around spouting negative thoughts. It wasn't the right mind-set.

"Talk, or I'll do what I wanted to do on the train," she threatened.

One of his eyes opened slightly so he could peer out at her. "Which was?"

"Scream and throw things," she said honestly.

"Why?" The other eye opened.

"Because you were being so darned polite."

"I thought that was what you wanted."

"It was—is—it's just a little hard to get used to, that's all."

"Yeah. Tell me about it." Eric grimaced. "I thought for sure, once you and I were on the carousel, you'd remember."

Her nostrils flared, her breathing suddenly shallow and rapid. "Remember what?"

He closed his eyes again and held her hand more tightly. "The time when we snuck off to Heritage Park with that bunch of other kids from the horse show. God, what a day. We had such a great time. I couldn't believe you didn't remember it."

"But I did." Mary saw his eyes pop open. They weren't the same eyes that had closed moments before. These green eyes held fire and passion—and anger.

"You lied? When I think of all I went through today to jog your memory..."

"I thought *you'd* forgotten."

"I had. But when it all came back to me, it did it with a vengeance."

"I see." Giving a tug, Mary reclaimed her hand. "That's too bad."

"Yeah. I agree. Feelings like those are best left in the past where they belong." He got to his feet. "Well, I'd better be going. Thanks for the aspirin."

Mary stared after him. He was leaving? She'd just admitted that she remembered a romantic afternoon they'd shared and he was leaving? What was the matter with him? More importantly, what was the matter with her that he didn't want to stay and revive those old memories?

The click of the latch echoed in the silence. Mary leaned back. Without Eric, the room seemed cold and empty. Just like her life.

"Is he gone?" Hope climbed over the back of the couch and slid down next to her mother.

"Looks like it."

"Good," the little girl said. "'Cause I want to ask you somethin' real important."

"Oh?" Mary turned and curled one leg under her so she could face Hope. "Like what?"

"It's about fathers. Real ones, I mean."

"I told you about your father."

"Oh, I don't mean *him*," Hope explained patiently. She scowled. "I just want you to tell me what it's like to have a daddy all the time."

"I'm probably the wrong person to ask," Mary said. "My parents and I didn't get along very well."

"Didn't they love you?"

"Of course they loved me."

"Did you love them?"

The question was a natural one. Voicing the honest answer was the rough part. "Yes. It was hard sometimes, though."

"How come?"

The insight and candor with which Hope approached the subject amazed Mary. For a long time she'd told herself that the reason she remained estranged from her parents was that they'd rejected Hope. That was true, up to a point, but it wasn't the only reason. Evidently, part of her still thought like a headstrong teenager; a case of arrested development if she'd ever seen one.

"I guess I got used to assuming they were doing things only to spite me," Mary said, her heart heavy. "That wasn't very fair, was it?"

"Nope." Hope got to her feet, ending their discussion. "Where are we going for dinner?"

"You're hungry?"

"Sure. Starved."

"How about room service?" Mary was having trouble concentrating on Hope's empty stomach when her empty heart demanded so many answers. She'd thought a lot about families and about her parents lately. Maybe it was time she tried to open the lines of communication, as Katie had urged.

"Ugh. I hate room service," Hope told her. "How about calling Uncle John?" She snatched up the telephone receiver and dialed his room, holding the earpiece out so Mary could hear the unanswered ringing. "He's not home."

"Probably not. I imagine he thought we'd eat with Eric."

"We could do that!" She dialed again before Mary could stop her. "Hi! Want to go out to dinner?" Giggling, she passed the phone to Mary. "He wants to know who I am."

Mary took the receiver. If she didn't act soon on her decision to contact her parents, the urge would probably pass unheeded, as it had before. This time, she really did want to write the long-overdue letter of healing.

She sighed. "Hello, Eric. Sorry to bother you but do you suppose you could take Hope out for a bite to eat?"

"What about you?" he asked, sounding concerned.

"I've decided to write to my folks and I'd like some time alone. Hope says she's hungry and I thought—"

"I'll be right over."

"No arguments?" Mary realized he'd been acting overly cooperative lately, but the ease with which he granted her request still surprised her. "You don't have to, you know."

"Yes, I do. How long has it been since you last wrote to your parents?" He knew the answer, via Katie and John, but wanted Mary to put it into words so she could hear herself speak it.

"About seven years," she said, her voice wavering. "I hope I can do it right after all this time."

"Say what's in your heart," he advised. "That's all anyone needs to do."

She snorted with derision. "You don't know my parents."

Eric's voice was gentle, his words carefully chosen. "After all this time, Mary, you probably don't know them, either."

Seven drafts of the letter lay crumpled in the wastepaper basket, along with enough tear-dampened tissues to half fill the receptacle. Mary rose to pace the floor, the last version in her hand. This one was probably as good as it was ever going to get. Not that she'd read the whole thing at once. Every time she tried, her weeping started anew, and she had yet to make it through the entire letter without pausing to blow her nose.

A soft knock on the door came as she was about to try again. It was Eric, bearing the sleeping little girl in his arms. He stepped inside while Mary held the door.

"She conked out on the ride home," he said. "I didn't have the heart to wake her. She's had a long day."

"So have we," Mary said. "Carry her to bed and I'll undress her later."

He stopped to study her puffy eyes and the paper she clutched in her hand. "You wrote it?"

"Sort of." Mary tried to smile and found it wasn't too hard to do, now that Eric had returned.

Following him into Hope's room, she removed the child's shoes while Eric pulled a coverlet over her. Then she picked up her letter and led the way back into the sitting room.

"Would you like me to mail that for you?" he asked.

"No. I mean, I'm not sure it's ready."

Eric stepped closer. "Was it that hard to write?" His hand cupped her cheek, his thumb tenderly tracing the redness below her eyes.

"Harder." Mary turned her back to him, leaning closer as his hands began to caress her upper arms. "I couldn't forget how they kept telling me I'd ruined their special plans for me. I was their only child and they'd pinned all their hopes on me. I was supposed to become a world champion, but Hope came along and I never made it."

"That was a long time ago, Mary. Time heals."

"Do you really think so?"

Her breath was a shudder and he held her closer, drawing his forearms across her chest and nestling her hips into the hollow of his. "Yes."

"Suppose I spoil everything by saying too much in the letter?" she asked. "I'm not so sure I didn't overdo it."

"It'll be fine. I told you what to say."

She turned within the circle of his arms. "No. You told me to speak the truth, and that may be too strong for them." Her reddened eyes searched his. "Read it for me, Eric? Tell me if you think it's okay."

"Are you sure?" Touched, he nevertheless wanted her to be absolutely certain of her decision before she bared her soul for him to see.

"I'm sure. I can't show it to Uncle John or Aunt Katie because they don't know the truth about Hope. You're the only one who does know, besides my parents. You're the logical one to choose."

"All right." He accepted the letter and stepped away from her. That she wrote it at all was the first miracle. That she wanted him to see it was the second—a miracle hinting at trust and perhaps even love. He was more than flattered that she'd asked his opinion. He was awed.

Mary watched him settle himself into the chair at the writing desk, lean forward to catch the light and begin to scan the page. Soon, his carefully neutral expression transformed until she couldn't believe her eyes.

She stared. There was no doubt about it. The muscles in Eric's jaw clenched, his hands became fists and the moist glint in his eyes increased until a tear rose over the rim of his lower eyelid and slid down his cheek toward the paper.

Chapter Thirteen

"You hurt that much?" Eric whispered, looking up at her.

"That much."

"The worst part must have been being forced to leave the States." Laying the letter aside, he came toward her and enfolded her in his embrace. "I'm so sorry."

She slid her arms around his waist, accepting the comfort he offered, giving comfort of her own. "No. The worst part was feeling so alone."

"And then Hope was born?"

"And then Hope was born." Mary laid her cheek on his chest. "She's everything to me."

Eric kissed the top of her head, breathing in the sweet scent of her hair. "It doesn't have to be that way. Everyone needs a family. Hope needs a father."

"I know that."

Eric stiffened. Was it really going to be this easy? "You do?"

"Yes. I've been giving it a lot of thought lately, thanks to you."

Joy sang along his nerves and filled every crevice of his soul. There really were such things as miracles, and he was living in the midst of one! "And?"

"And I've decided not to try to wait till Hope is grown before I consider matrimony. As soon as I get back home, I'll go shopping, so to speak."

His gut tied in a knot the size of a Texas watermelon. He didn't like the glazed-over look in Mary's eyes one bit.

"Shopping for what? Explain." He held her away so he could look fully into her face. Had he been such a gentleman that she'd misunderstood his motives, his feelings? Surely she must know how much he cared about her in spite of his careful courting.

"For an Irish husband, of course."

"You're joking." She *had* to be.

Mary shook her head. "No. I'm serious."

"You can't be." Releasing her, Eric turned to walk across the room, then wheeled to face her. "What about me? What about Hope? Surely..."

"I've thought that all through," Mary told him with more calm assurance than she'd felt for weeks. She was looking forward to the return of some long-overdue, happily dull stability to her life. "You'll continue to be welcome when you visit, of course. I wouldn't take that away from you."

"How kind of you." Eric's temper was stampeding out of control and he didn't try to subdue it. Not this time. He was through pretending and doing things Mary's way. "This mythical husband of yours had better be very understanding. Do you intend to tell him that I'm the man who made passionate love to you on a bed of straw and created our daughter, or are you simply going to let him see the longing in my eyes every time I look at you, and figure out for himself that I'm madly in love with you?''

"Don't say that!''

In four strides he was within reach once again. He grasped her shoulders as if in preparation to shake her, but instead simply trembled with rage. "Why not? It's true and you know it.''

"No, it isn't. Let me go, Eric.''

"Not until I've made you think,'' he said, struggling to forget his faceless, nameless rival long enough to speak coherently. "Don't you know what you do to me? What you *are* to me?''

"I know.''

"Then how can you even consider...''

She shushed him by placing her fingertips on his lips. When he kissed them, she melted against him. "It isn't you, Eric,'' she breathed into the charged stillness. "It's what you do, where you go, who you've become. Writing to my parents tonight brought it all back to me. You're famous. A world traveler. A celebrity in equine circles. I want no part of that kind of existence again, for me or for my daughter, and I'm not foolish enough to ask you to change. You are what you are. So am I. We don't belong together. Chances are, we never did.''

"You're afraid.''

Looking deeply into her eyes, Eric saw that he was at least partially right. Behind the impassioned excuses lay fear as well as firm commitment to her decision. One or the other, he might be able to overcome. Against both her trepidation and her iron will, he could see he stood little chance.

"I'm only concerned for Hope,'' Mary said. "She's an intelligent kid but she's also overly sensitive. Why do you think I've been so adamant about protecting her from my vindictive parents?''

"You're running away from love." His lips descended to brush a light kiss over hers. "I understand how those feelings might frighten you. Hell, they scare the wits out of me, but you can't deny what's happened between us the past few weeks."

Mary clung to him in a last goodbye, her eyes filling with new tears. "I don't deny it, Eric, I just see no future in it for us."

He tilted her head up so he could search her eyes for the answers he wanted even if her lips told him otherwise. It was all there for anyone to see. Mary did love him.

"Say it, anyway," he urged. "Tell me you love me."

"What good will that do?"

His jaw clenched. "Tell me. Say it. Say, 'I love you, Eric.' Go on."

Mary felt his intense passion flowing through her, becoming a part of her. All her determination fled in the presence of his overpowering yearning. Even without his forceful words, the look in his eyes would have penetrated her defenses all the way to her soul. Speaking of his love so boldly, Eric had gone deeper into her heart than she'd ever thought possible. And the wrenching of their parting was going to hurt more than anything in her wildest imaginings.

Her lips parted, quivering. He was still waiting for her words, the words he'd commanded, the words that until now she'd spoken only into the empty stillness of night.

Mary managed a tender, tearful smile. "It won't make any difference. My mind is made up."

"I don't care." He shook his head. "I need to hear it."

"Then, I love you, Eric Lambert."

In the quiet, he answered softly, "I love you, too."

Mary hadn't intended her confession to be an invitation to passion but that was the effect it had on Eric. Scooping her up in his arms, he carried her to the couch and lowered her gently onto the cushions, her head coming to rest on the arm.

Visions of a bed of fresh straw flashed through her mind. No longer were they two novices, falling unexpectedly into each other's arms. They were adults. They knew what they were doing, and heaven help her, Mary wanted him as badly as his expression said he wanted her.

Wordlessly, he lowered himself to lie beside her, his lips pulling gently at hers until she parted them for the explorations of his tongue, his sweet, sweet ragged breath.

Stop him, her conscience prompted. But the sense of déjà vu, of rightness, was too strong. This was the man who had taught her about love, the only one whose arms fit around her perfectly, whose presence banished the loneliness that lingered forever at the fringes of her consciousness.

It isn't fair, she thought, reaching out to him and wrapping her arms around him to pull him closer. Life isn't fair. It never has been.

Mary clung to him in desperate need of solace as well as physical release. A long, difficult quest lay ahead of her. Somehow, she'd have to find a man worthy of taking Eric's place; someone as loving, as gentle, as passionate, and who also cared as deeply about Hope's future. It was an enormous challenge, one she doubted she could surmount. And if not, her heart warned, if not, you'll be alone again. Forever.

She held him more tightly, feeling his heartbeat beside hers. His hand caressed her back, then drifted down over the curve of her hip. She shuddered. Eric. How she did love him! And how unfair it was to encourage his lovemaking when she knew there was no possible future for their love.

Gathering every shred of her self-control, she mustered just enough to whisper his name. "Eric?"

With a sigh, he levered over her. His nostrils were flared, his eyes filled with longing and adoration.

"Eric, we mustn't do this."

The answer he gave surprised her. "I know."

Slipping off the edge of the couch, he knelt beside her and took her hands, bringing them to his lips and kissing them before speaking again. "I told myself I wouldn't make the same mistake twice."

"So did I." She managed a feeble smile. "It's easier to make a promise like that when we're not together, isn't it?"

"Yeah." Still breathing hard, he rocked back on his heels. "Lots easier."

In his eyes there were unasked questions. Mary knew they should talk in spite of the fact that such a discussion would probably mean an end to the touching, the kissing, the belonging she coveted so.

"I've given my future a lot of thought," she finally said. "I want you to understand, the decisions I made weren't easy ones, even when I thought you'd given up on me."

His grip on her slim fingers tightened. "And you're sure? There's no chance for us?"

Eric cursed the moisture gathering in his eyes. Damn it all. He was a man and men didn't cry. Ever. He looked at Mary, noting the fresh moisture in her eyes, too. If she began to weep, he was likely to lose control completely and disgrace himself more than he already had. It was bad enough that she was rejecting him for good—he couldn't let her take the last shred of his tattered pride with her, too.

To break the spell of the moment, he rose quickly and paced across the room, waving his arms in the air. "How can I change your mind? What can I do that I haven't already done?" The volume and tone of his voice expressed more strident, poignant emotion than he wanted, but it was beyond his control. He was lucky he could speak at all, considering the way he was feeling.

Mary sat up. Straightening her clothes, she tossed her hair back and got to her feet. "Nothing. There's nothing either you or I can do."

The sleepy, squeaky voice that cut the ensuing silence brought both adults up short. "Mama? What's wrong?" Hope rubbed her eyes. "Why are you and Eric so mad at each other?"

"We're not mad, honey," Mary said, going to her and hugging her.

"Then why is Eric yelling?" Pulling away from her mother, the sleepy child padded on stocking feet to the man she'd grown to love and tugged on his hand until he bent down for his customary hug.

With one arm still around his neck, Hope looked back at her mother. "Why can't Eric be my father all the time, like today?"

"He..." Mary couldn't find the words to explain.

Kindly, patiently, Eric spoke to Hope. "To make that wish come true I'd have to marry your mother, honey, and she says she doesn't want that to happen."

"Why not?" Hope clung more tightly to his neck and he picked her up.

"Because she has other, different plans for her life. Grown-ups have to make hard decisions like that sometimes."

"But, why?"

Eric sought an explanation the child could relate to her experiences. "It's like when you're training a new horse," he said. "Sometimes the hurdles look very big and dangerous, so the horse doesn't want to jump. He's scared because he's never tried it before and he's afraid he won't be able to do it. If you try to force him, he can fall and hurt himself and hurt you, too. See?"

"I don't know. I guess so." Hope snuggled against his shoulder and he stroked her hair.

"Well, it's kind of like that with me and your mother. She didn't have a lot of happy family times when she was young so she's not sure it's a good idea to get married right now."

"How about later?" Hope offered, perking up. "You could come visit us again and she could think about it then."

"I will. I promise." Still carrying her, Eric started back for Hope's room. "And you need to promise me you'll try very hard to love a new daddy if she finds you somebody else."

The child's eyes widened and she looked up at him in the dimness of the unlit bedroom. "You mean, besides you?"

He swallowed hard. "Yes. Besides me." Lowering her onto the bed, he bent to kiss her forehead as he tucked the blankets around her.

"I don't want to promise that," the child said honestly.

Eric straightened, glad for the cover of the darkness. The only light in the room was from the doorway behind him, and he was thankful Hope couldn't see his face in the shadows or make out the telltale moisture streaking his cheeks.

"I won't make you promise, then," he said quietly. "You just think about it, okay? We both want your mama to be happy, don't we?" He smoothed back her tousled hair.

"Yes."

"Then that's all that counts. Sleep tight. And if we don't run into each other tomorrow, have a safe trip home." The light from the doorway illuminated her face and he could see that she'd already closed her eyes.

Angry at his weakness, he swiped at his sparse tears, cursing their presence, and placed a last goodbye kiss on Hope's brow. What he'd told her was the pure truth and it had helped focus his thoughts. He did want Mary to be happy, and if that meant he had to get out of her life, then he would. It was as simple as that.

Once more, he gazed down at the sleeping angel he'd given life to. She deserved a father—a real father—not someone simply playing the part when it was convenient for him, a guy who showed up between competitions or whenever he happened to be on her side of the Atlantic. If he fell into that role, he'd be doing them all a disservice.

No. Hope needed a live-in, there-when-you-needed-him, ever-present father. And Mary was right. He wasn't that man. He lived in California and Mary loved Ireland. He traveled and Mary wanted to stay home. He would want to nurture the inherent talent and potential in Hope and then urge her to compete, while Mary hated everything about the sport except the horses themselves.

Eric felt his calm and self-possession returning. No matter what his heart told him, he didn't belong in Mary's life.

Leaning his head back he took a deep breath and closed his eyes for a moment, searching for peace, calling forth the precise control that was his stock in trade. Tomorrow, he would compete, then make his apologies to John for leaving early and fly home as if he didn't care about anything but his work. It would be the hardest thing he'd ever done.

It would be his wedding gift to Mary.

Mary's idea of a good disguise was the largest, darkest pair of sunglasses she could buy. They seemed to work, because no one in the stands or at the colorful, outdoor Festival of Nations took the slightest notice of her.

Mr. O'Malley jumped well, but not well enough, even with Eric as his rider. While winners of the preliminary rounds went on to the finals, Mary took Hope to the stables to see her old friend and stood aside while the horse nuzzled her and tried to put his big, soft nose into her pockets.

"He's looking for more cookies," Mary remarked. "You've spoiled him something awful."

Hope giggled as he snuffled her hair. "I know. Poor Mr. O'Malley. He did try so hard. Didn't he?"

"That he did." She looked to John. "It was a good showing in spite of the loss."

"I know." Taking off his cap he fingered the brim and cleared his throat. "I, uh, I have a message for you."

"Not the Slones! Please tell me you haven't seen them again." Mary glanced quickly right and left. She'd taken care to avoid the barns and the trade-show buildings as much as possible, and as soon as Hope was through fawning over the chestnut she intended to sprint for the peace and quiet of their rooms.

"No," John said. "Not them. The message is from Eric."

So that was why she didn't see him nearby. Ever since he'd turned so stiffly formal and left her suite the night before, she'd been dreading their next meeting. Obviously, so had he. It was hard enough to talk to him when they were on amiable terms, and judging from his most recent behavior, they weren't exactly bosom buddies anymore.

Mary managed a smile and a nod. "Go ahead."

"He said to tell you goodbye."

"Goodbye?"

John cocked his head at the hotel in the distant background. "I imagine he's packing right now. He's planning on heading back to the States as soon as possible."

"I see." She felt her heart drop all the way to her stomach, flip over and come to rest as a giant lump in her throat.

"He also said it may be a long while before he gets back to Ireland."

She shaded her eyes, ostensibly from the brightness of the sun in spite of her dark glasses, and turned away to look out over the crowd. "Hope will be really disappointed to hear that, I'm afraid. She thought Eric was the best thing alive, next to Mr. O'Malley, of course."

"If you want to go tell him goodbye in person, I can look after Hope for you."

"No. That won't be necessary. Eric sort of said goodbye to Hope and me last night." Turning away, she remembered the letter languishing in her purse. Whether or not her parents read it or responded to it, it should be mailed, for everyone's sake. That, she could do with no regrets. And then she, too, would make plans to go home.

Thinking of her cottage and the beautiful farm on which it was built brought a catch to her throat. It was home, as no other place had ever been, with its quaint charm and country antique furnishings. She saw it all in vivid detail. And within its walls, a permanent part of it all, there was the vision of Eric, running his fingers over the stones in the hearth, eating at her table, laughing about cookie crumbs and lint. Home was her last stronghold, the only true bastion of asylum she had, and Eric's memory was all around and through it now, too. She might as well accept it. There was no place she could hide where he wouldn't be, at least in spirit.

The only option left was to escape into herself, the way she had when she was a lonely child. But one glance into her heart told her what she already knew. Eric Lambert waited for her there, too.

Chapter Fourteen

Eric's answering machine gave him more information than the simple message John Day had left. The tone of voice told Eric the man was worried. He immediately put everything else aside and dialed overseas.

"Ah, Eric! Good. I was waiting for your call."

He gripped the receiver. "What is it? What's wrong? It isn't Hope? She hasn't been hurt?"

"No, no. Nothing like that."

Eric sank into a chair. "Thank God. Then, what?"

"It's Mary," John said.

With his heart pounding so hard he could feel it in his throat, Eric choked out, "Mary? What happened to Mary?"

John made a disgusted sound. "Plenty. She's actually thinkin' of marryin' that blithering idiot, O'Malley."

"Oh, God. So soon?" Eric slumped down.

"So soon? Did you know about this?"

"She told me she wanted a nice, settled, Irish husband," Eric said dispassionately, "but I never dreamed she'd act on the idea so fast."

"Well, she hasn't, exactly," John explained. "She told Katie she was considering O'Malley. Katie got all dithered and told me. That's why I'm callin'."

Eric sighed. "I don't know what you expect me to do about it, John. I've already told her I loved her and asked her to marry me."

"Well, what did she say? Does she love you?"

"Oh, yeah. She loves me, all right. There's just nothing else about me she likes. I was hoping maybe if she made up with her parents, she'd be more open to living the kind of life she used to. With me."

"There's not much of a chance of that, I'm afraid. Her letter came back unopened."

"Dear Lord. Poor Mary."

"Aye. She took it hard. It was right after that she started talkin' about being wed."

"I suppose O'Malley is bragging to every man in the pub." Eric could picture the revelry and ensuing celebration, before and after the fateful marriage.

"No. The dolt has no idea how close he is to matrimony. Mary hasn't had the nerve to tell him yet. I suppose that's just as well."

"She hasn't?" For the first time since their disturbing conversation had begun, Eric was starting to feel encouraged.

"No." John paused. "And I can't help thinkin' it's because she really doesn't want to do it."

"The only profession I know well is horses and competition," Eric said by way of explanation. "It's been my whole life. Once I start the breeding program you and I planned, I won't have to travel as much as I used to, but there will still be the same connections to the past that Mary hates so."

"I know, son."

"So, what am I going to do?"

"You're running in the backfield—a real longshot, all right."

"Longshots sometimes win," Eric said.

"They can if they don't give up in the homestretch," John reminded him wisely.

"I've never quit in my life."

"I thought not. So, what are we going to do now?"

Chuckling, Eric leaned back in the chair. "We? Hell, I don't know. You're Irish. You bragged that you learned to handle women from your father and his father, before him. You tell me."

"Well, I may have been exaggerating a bit."

"Naw. Not you." He sobered. "What *am* I going to do, John? I love her so much I can hardly get through the days, and the nights are pure hell."

"Then come back to Ireland, son. Face her. In the meantime, I'll see if I can't talk her into getting away from the farm for a while so you can meet on neutral ground. After that, it's up to you."

"Thanks a bunch. Some romantic adviser *you* turned out to be."

"You're quite welcome. Anytime. Phone when you have your airline ticket and I'll tell you what's happened with us up to then."

"All right." Pausing, Eric began to smile. "And, John..."

"Yes?"

"Thanks. I'll never forget this."

"You sure as the devil better not. I'll expect a grand and glorious present from you and your family every Christmas and a trip to the pub with you on my birthday—all expenses paid.''

"Done." Eric chuckled. "You sound confident that I'll be able to convince her to change her mind.''

"I'm bettin' on the best man I know for the job, son. I always do.''

"I am, you know. I'll make her happy. I swear I will.''

It was John's turn to laugh. "If I didn't think so, Mr. Lambert, we wouldn't be havin' this conversation. Oh, by the way, she finally got up the nerve to tell Katie and me that she was never married. I thought she was going to drop over in a dead faint when we confessed that we'd already figured as much. One thing led to another and your name was mentioned.''

"Uh-oh.''

"Yeah. Remember how I told you she'd gotten all flustered, seeing you on TV?''

"Yes.''

"Well, she was pretty steamed when I told her I'd gotten my original idea to contact you that day, because I'd guessed there had to have been somethin' between you two once. All along, she'd figured she was hidin' her reactions perfectly when in reality, they stood out like a lighthouse beacon.''

"Is she still mad?" Eric asked.

"Doesn't seem to be." John snorted. "Surprised the hell out of me, but it looks like she's forgiven me for my meddling.''

"Does she know you're still at it?''

"Not likely. But she's a bright girl. She'll realize I've acted for the best. You'll see.''

"I hope so." Eric bid him goodbye and hung up the phone.

He had his ticket to Ireland in his hand within the hour.

* * *

Killarney National Park in County Kerry was twenty thousand acres in all, so if John hadn't tipped Eric to the fact that Mary was taking Hope to see the nineteenth-century Elizabethan-style manor house and grounds, he might never have found her.

He'd spent the entire previous day strolling the carefully manicured gardens and waiting and watching, but she hadn't appeared as predicted. A quick call to John confirmed that she was, indeed, still coming, although later than first thought.

In desperation and frustration, Eric took another ride in a jaunting cart. It was a one-horse affair, open on top to best display the magnificent view, and very old-country in design with two large wheels and unpadded bench seats. Eric figured it was better to be doing something, even if he had heard the tourist-oriented speech before, than to pace the walkways aimlessly until Mary finally arrived.

"You sure must love this place," the carriage master said. "Didn't I carry you around it yesterday, too?"

Eric looked at him closely. "I guess it was you." He scooted forward and offered his hand. "The name's Eric Lambert."

The driver turned to shake hands. "They call me Michael. Till you spoke, I'd have taken you for one of us. Nice cap and jacket you've got there." He touched the worn brim of his own hat. "Me, now, I like to be comfortable."

"I'm trying to fit in over here," Eric admitted, straightening his tweed coat and smoothing the wool of his slacks. "You really think this is okay?"

"That, I do. What brings you to Killarney?"

It had been a long, tiring flight, and since his arrival he'd had little chance for more than a few words with John. The opportunity to talk candidly to another man appealed to him enough to cause him to speak his mind.

"I've come to win the hand of a stubborn woman," he said with a wry smile. "Any advice?"

"She's Irish?"

"Californian by birth. Irish by heritage."

"Still, that's probably bad enough. Our women can be a bit hardheaded sometimes."

"Tell me about it!" Leaning back in the seat behind the driver's left shoulder, Eric stretched. "I'm so darned tense I may never be normal again. I envy you, getting to drive the horse like you do."

"You like these beasties, do you?"

"Love 'em. I usually ride, though."

"Well, hop up here beside me and you can take Nell's reins. She knows the route through the gardens and down by the lake so well she wouldn't need me along if it wasn't for my gift of gab. I haven't taught her to talk, as yet."

"Thanks." Eric did as Michael suggested.

"Is your lady comin' here?"

"So I'm told." He clucked to the mare and she stepped along.

"Killarney's pretty, all right, but I've seen more romantic, private places, if you know what I mean."

"I do." Eric smiled. "She'll have a little girl with her, too, though, so this park will have to do."

"Ah, I see. And when will she be gettin' here?"

"Last I heard, not before this afternoon."

"You aim to surprise her?"

"That was my plan."

"She'll be glad to see you, will she?" They turned down a shaded lane beneath a canopy of oak, birch and ash trees and followed the banks of a lake where black-and-white

wans glided gracefully across the water and tiny brown-
and-gray birds darted above.

"She'll be surprised," Eric said. "Though I'm not sure
how glad she'll be to see me."

The carriage master tilted back his cap and scratched his
head. "And you came *how* far to see this girl?"

Eric told him. "About six thousand miles."

"Whew! She must really be something."

"She is," Eric said, smiling. "Oh, yes, she certainly is."
He cocked his head, an idea forming. "Say, would you
consider trading jackets and hats and renting me this fine
jaunting cart for the afternoon?"

"Mama, I want to ride in the carts!" Hope tugged on
Mary's hand, dragging her closer.

It was then that Eric caught the little girl's eye. He was up
on the driver's seat of the third cart in line in front of the
vine-covered mansion, Michael's old, battered cap partially obscuring his face. As Hope opened her mouth to call
to him, he laid his index finger across his lips, shushing her.
Pointing to the cart he was driving, he saw the clever child
nod.

"I changed my mind, Mama. I like the brown-and-white
horse on that other cart the best."

"We have to take the next one in line," Mary told her.
"These men make their livings from tourists and they take
turns."

Hope looked up at the people behind them and pointed.
"You go ahead. My mama and I want the cart with the
pretty horse. Over there." She beamed at Mary. "Okay?"

Beyond argument, Mary let herself be shepherded to the
cart Hope had chosen. It didn't matter to her if they took
this cart, that cart or no cart. She'd only agreed to make this
trip as a favor to Hope. School would be starting soon and

John had gotten the poor kid all excited about an outing to Killarney before he'd been called away on business, leaving Mary to carry out his plans for him.

Truth be told, Mary didn't care where she was. The beautiful countryside she'd always loved seemed drab and dull. Her life had gone from a kaleidoscope of color to flat black and white when she'd made up her mind to put Eric out of her life. Or gray, she decided. That was it. Gray.

She drew her coat around her as she climbed into the cart. At least Hope was happy—finally. She'd pouted and sulked so much after she learned that Eric had left Calgary ahead of them that she'd been a holy terror to live with.

Not that Mary had been much better, she acknowledged ruefully. In that aspect of her behavior, Hope had the right idea. Without Eric, nothing was nearly as much fun as it had been.

I'll get over it, Mary had told herself again and again, as if the thinking of it would make it so. But it hadn't. Nearly a month had passed and she still missed him so badly she was hardly civil to anyone, least of all herself.

The carriage driver's thick Irish brogue droned on in the background, its tones reminding her of Eric's voice the same way everything she heard, saw, smelled or tasted reminded her of him. He was everywhere. And nowhere.

"The castle had a moat in those oul days," he said. "But they ran out of crocodiles, so they filled it up."

Hope giggled and Mary tapped her knee to shush her.

"Yes, siree. 'Twas a sad sight. When Saint Patrick drove out all the snakes, those poor crocs went right along, as easy as you please, and never were seen again."

"Really," Mary said, sounding miffed. "If you don't know the real history of this place, I'd rather you didn't make up stories and confuse the poor child."

The driver touched the brim of his cap and hunched forward more, rounding his shoulders. "So, 'tis the truth you'll be wanting?"

"Of course." Mary squinted at Hope, who had all but fallen off the seat in a fit of giggling.

Drawing the horse to a halt with a loud "Whoa," he kept his back to his passengers. "In that case..."

He climbed down, rounded the cart and stood facing the open back at Mary's feet. "In that case," he repeated, removing his hat, "I love you, Mary Mulraney. Put me out of my misery. Marry me."

"Eric!" Brightly colored lights flashed behind Mary's eyes and the trees above seemed to sway crazily although there was no wind, not even a breeze. Obviously, Uncle John had been up to his old tricks and was playing matchmaker again. Boy, was he going to get a piece of her mind when she got home! That, and maybe a big hug, to boot— *after* she told him off. The old stinker. She blinked hard to assure herself she wasn't hallucinating, that Eric was really there.

He bowed. "The Irish version of me, at your service. According to Michael, the man who really owns this cart, I fit right in."

"Yes!" Hope shouted. "Oh, yes, Eric. We'll marry you!" She launched herself at him, grabbed his neck and laughed as he swung her around and around, high off the ground.

"Hope Mulraney!" Mary wasn't sure whether she should laugh or cry, or both. Dear Lord, Eric looked good to her. And seeing him with Hope again...

"Well, why not get married?" the girl insisted. "Whyever not?"

Mary completed the decision she'd toyed with for the last month. It wasn't fair to keep deceiving Hope about her parentage. Originally, it had seemed the right choice but now it was clear it had been a mistake to lie. She'd found that out when she'd confessed her past sins to John and Katie and they'd been so understanding, so supportive in spite of everything. No wonder John had set her up like this. How could she stay mad at him when, in her heart of hearts, she blessed him for his loving meddling?

She held out her hand to Hope. "Come here, honey."

The child came quickly when Eric set her down, and hopped back up on the seat beside Mary. In everyone's actions there was caution and excitement, as if all sensed a momentous event was about to occur.

Mary took Hope's small hands and looked into her Lambert-green eyes. "A long time ago, when we were very young, Eric and I fell in love. It wasn't right for us to get married then, but we did have a baby. A little girl. You." She paused so the shock could set in, but was startled to see absolutely no adverse reaction reflected in Hope's face. "So, you see, Eric is your real daddy, after all."

The child began to grin as she glanced at Eric, then looked back at her mother. "Cool. I'd of picked him, anyway. Now, will you get married?"

Wide-eyed, Mary looked to Eric. He, too, was grinning. Like father, like daughter. "Oh, for heaven's sake," Mary muttered, sinking back against the cart seat. "You're both incorrigible."

"Can you handle the reins for us?" he asked Hope. When she nodded wildly, he boosted her over into the driver's seat. "This is Nell. She knows the way. Just take your time. I have a lot to say to your mother."

"Yes, Daddy."

He chucked her under the chin. Climbing in beside Mary, he clasped her hands in his. "I've never done this the way I'd rehearsed it. It always seems to pop out in the condensed version, but I do love you and I do want to marry you. I can't promise I'll give up the competition circuit entirely, though, unless you're willing to starve to death with me. Horses are my profession. I'm afraid I wouldn't be very successful behind a desk in some office."

"Oh, Lord, no!" Mary looked deep into his eyes. "You must never consider doing that."

"If that was the only way I could have you, I would."

She smiled at him. "Well, Mr. Lambert, you're in luck, because I've decided to put you out of your misery, like you wanted."

"You're going to shoot me?"

"No." She giggled, her nervousness growing in spite of having finally made the decision her heart had insisted on all along. "I'm going to marry you."

Hope cheered so loudly that Nell jumped ahead and started to trot, but the girl slowed her easily.

"It was the hat and coat, wasn't it?" Eric teased, so happy he wasn't making much sense. "That was what did it for me. My authentic Irish costume."

Laughing, Mary patted his cheek. "No, dear one. It's what's underneath." When he blushed, she explained. "It's not what's on the outside. It never was. 'Tis your lovin' heart that won me."

Eric pulled her into his arms. "Of all the successes I've ever had, you're the only one I care about," he whispered. "You and Hope. We'll be a great family."

Mary snuggled closer. For once, she agreed with him completely.

* * * * *

SMYTHESHIRE,
MASSACHUSETTS.

Small town. Big secrets.

**Silhouette Romance invites you to visit Elizabeth August's
intriguing small town, a place with an unusual legacy
rooted deep in the past....**

THE VIRGIN WIFE (#921) February 1993
HAUNTED HUSBAND (#922) March 1993
LUCKY PENNY (#945) June 1993
A WEDDING FOR EMILY (#953) August 1993

Elizabeth August's SMYTHESHIRE, MASSACHUSETTS—
This sleepy little town has plenty to keep you up at night.
Only from Silhouette Romance!

HE'S MORE THAN A MAN, HE'S ONE OF OUR

Fabulous Fathers

DAD GALAHAD
by Suzanne Carey

Confirmed bachelor Ned Balfour hadn't thought of himself as a knight in shining armor—until he met Jenny McClain. The damsel in distress had turned to Ned for help, and his sense of duty wouldn't let him disappoint the fair maiden. Jenny's baby needed a father and he vowed to become that man, even though mother and child would surely disrupt his solitary life. Could this ready-made family be the answer to Ned's quest for happiness?

Find out who does the true rescuing in Suzanne Carey's DAD GALAHAD. Available in April—only from Silhouette Romance!

Fall in love with our FABULOUS FATHERS—and join the Silhouette Romance family!

Silhouette
ROMANCE™

FF493

Take 4 bestselling love stories FREE

Plus get a FREE surprise gift!

**Three All-American beauties discover
love comes in all shapes and sizes!**

ALL-AMERICAN SWEETHEARTS

by Laurie Paige

CARA'S BELOVED (#917)—*February*
SALLY'S BEAU (#923)—*March*
VICTORIA'S CONQUEST (#933)—*April*

A lost love, a new love and a hidden one, three *All-American
Sweethearts* get their men in Paradise Falls, West Virginia.
Only in America...and only from Silhouette Romance!

Silhouette
R O M A N C E™

COMING NEXT MONTH

#928 DAD GALAHAD—Suzanne Carey
Fabulous Fathers
It was Ned Balfour to the rescue for damsel in distress
Jenny McClain. Pregnant and alone, Jenny accepted Ned's
chivalrous offer of marriage, but could she trust this white
knight with her heart?

#929 WHO'S THAT BABY?—Kristin Morgan
Whitney Arceneaux was irresistibly drawn to both her new
neighbor, Garrett Scott, and his precious toddler. Yet there was
something *very* strange about this man—and the need she felt for
them both....

#930 LYON'S PRIDE—Maris Soule
Cartoonist Greg Lyon had taken a journey to find himself but
he discovered Dr. Amy Fraser instead. Though she'd cured his
injured leg with ease, he knew *he'd* have to be the one to mend
her heart.

#931 SORRY, WRONG NUMBER—Patricia Ellis
When a wrong number introduced Meg Porter to Nick Morgan, it
was a strong case of love on the line. But would Meg accept Nick
for who he really was, once they met face-to-face?

#932 THE RIGHT MAN—Marie Ferrarella
Leanne Sheridan had survived one bad marriage and was not
about to get involved with Cody Lancaster. Leanne's mind was
convinced Cody was all wrong for her...but her heart insisted he
was Mr. Right!

#933 VICTORIA'S CONQUEST—Laurie Paige
All-American Sweethearts
Lovely widow Victoria Broderick was intrigued by the depth of
passion Jason Broderick hid from the world. Now all she had to
do was make him admit his feelings for *her!*